MY BROTHER'S KEEPER

N. C. MANUEL

First printing April 2010

ISBN: 978-1-935591-12-2
ISBN: 1-935591-12-6

Printed by:
Grelin Press, PO Box 367
New Kensington, PA 15068
(724) 334-8240 grelinpress@aol.com
www.grelinpress.com

I would like to dedicate this book
to my son Meliki "Lil Bay Boe" Manley
and my niece Denazia Howard.
I have two hearts, one for each of you.
I love ya'll.

ACKNOWLEDGMENTS

I would like to acknowledge all the people who showed me love in the worst of times, as well as those who supported my vision and dream by helping me produce this book.

PROLOGUE

C-loc, Loco, and Blue all sat in the living room of C-loc's baby mom's house loading their guns up. They were getting ready to go meet one of their li'l locs who had a hot car they could use for a drive-by.

"Let's go handle this shit," C-loc said, sliding his fifty-shot clip into the chrome TEC-9 that he was carrying.

Blue was done loading his gun up as well, and he stood up ready to leave.

"Let's roll then," Loco said tucking his Uzi into his waist-band.

Before they could leave, Keisha, who was C-loc's girl, came strutting into the room, swinging her thick hips from side to side to attract the attention of his homies. "I know you ain't planning to leave after you said you was going to take me shopping. . . ." She was a firecracker and you could tell by the way she snapped her fingers and rolled her eyes that she meant business.

Instead of arguing with her, C-loc pulled out his money and peeled off a few hundreds. "Now don't spend this all in one place." He smiled as he handed her the money.

"I won't, baby," she said giving him a long kiss before going upstairs to get dress for a long day at the mall. She didn't know what she would do without C-loc in her life. Keisha counted out the thousand dollars he had given her, smiling at how lucky she was.

"Homie, she got you wide open, cuz," Loco said, shaking his head.

"I ain't open off that bitch, cuz. I just take care of her because she my son's mother."

When Blue heard him call Keisha a bitch, his blood began to boil. He hated how his old head disrespected her when she wasn't around. He felt that she would leave C-loc if she ever heard what he said about her. In his mind, Blue felt she deserved better, and if she were his, he would treat her like a queen. But it wasn't his place to say anything, so he just kept his mouth closed.

"So ya'll niggas ready, cuz?" Loco asked interrupting Blue's thoughts.

"Yeah, let's go," C-loc said heading to the front door. He saw the look that Blue made when he called his girl a bitch, and he was wondering what the problem was. Lately he even caught Blue staring at Keisha as if he wanted her. He smiled and thought to himself, *who wouldn't want to fuck her fine ass*?

As they walked around the corner to Femosa Street, Blue stopped and began to pat his pockets. "Damn. I forgot my mask and gloves."

"Run back to the house and grab them, because we can't have you getting knocked for leaving fingerprints or getting picked out of a line-up," Loco told him.

"Aiight, cuz. I'll be right back," he said as he began running back to C-loc's house. When he got there, he walked straight in as always. After looking around to make sure Keisha was still upstairs, he picked up the phone, but before he could dial the number, she came down the steps.

"What your young ass still doing in here?" she asked flirtatiously. She knew that Blue had a crush on her, and she liked to mess with his head every chance she got, even though she just looked at him as C-loc's young nigga. He didn't have a chance in hell at getting with her as long as her baby was around.

"I'm just trying to use the phone real quick," he said while looking her up and down. Couldn't nothing or nobody tell him that she wasn't feeling his style. He felt like the only reason he didn't have her was because of C-loc.

"Well, don't be long, because I'm about to leave out," she said turning around. When she looked back, his eyes were glued to her nice round ass, and she smiled to herself as she walked away, swaying her hips back and forth so hard that her ass jiggled through the jeans she was wearing.

"Lord have mercy," he said shaking his head after she left the room. Once she was gone, he began to dial the number into the phone and after five rings he got an answer.

"Who this?" the person on the other end of the call asked.

"It's Blue and I'm calling about that situation, so if you going to come through, then now is the time to do it."

"I'm already in the area, so good looking on the heads up."

"Just get at me when it's done and over with," Blue told the mysterious man.

"Say no more," the man said before breaking the connection.

*   *   *   *   *

Meanwhile, C-loc and Loco went into their mom's house to check on their seeds before going to handle their business. As soon as they opened the door, they could hear the boys arguing upstairs in their bedroom.

Loco looked at his mom, who was on the couch watching her soaps as if nothing was going on.

"Mom, why you ain't trying to stop them from fighting?" C-loc asked smiling.

"Break them up for what, when all they going to do is go right back at it when I leave them alone. Ya'll need to sit them down and talk to them."

"Yeah, you right," Loco said, walking to the bottom of the steps. "Brandon...CJ...come down here!" he hollered.

At the sound of his voice, the arguing stopped. They knew that their dads didn't like them arguing, and they thought that they were in big trouble.

"I know ya'll hear me up there," Loco said. He was ready to go up the steps and punish them if they didn't reply.

Brandon's head popped up around the corner and his eyes were lit up. "What's up, Dad?" he asked.

"Go get your brother and come downstairs," Loco told him.

When they came into the dining room, the boys were told to sit down at the table by their fathers.

"So why was ya'll fighting?" C-loc asked them.

"We wasn't fighting, Dad." CJ told the blatant lie with a straight face.

"We heard ya'll fighting. Now we not mad, but we want to know what ya'll were fighting about."

"He put my shoes on without asking," Brandon said trying to justify his actions.

"That's your brother, right?" his dad asked him.

"Yeah, Dad, but. . . ."

"Ain't no buts. If that's your brother, then what's yours is his and what's his is yours. Ya'll have to look out for each other, because ain't nobody else going to look out for ya'll. Understand?"

Both of the boys nodded their heads yes.

"Well, let your brother pick out whatever he want," Loco told Brandon.

"Aiight, Dad," Brandon said before giving him and C-loc a hug.

"And CJ, don't let me catch ya'll arguing again," his pops told him.

"Aiight, Dad," CJ said, hugging him and Loco.

After being chastised by their fathers, both of the boys headed back to their rooms, but before they got all the way up the steps, C-loc called them back down.

"What's up?" they both asked, walking into the dining room.

"Are you your brother's keeper?" C-loc asked CJ.

CJ knew what his dad wanted to hear, because he asked this question every time he and his brother were caught arguing. "Yes, I am," CJ replied.

"What about you? Are you your brother's keeper?" Loco asked Brandon.

Brandon knew that he was wrong for acting petty towards his brother. He felt a little guilty over the whole situation. He loved his brother and would not act funny towards him again. "Yes, I am," he told his dad, and he meant it with all of his heart.

"That's right. Ya'll are each other's keeper, and I don't want ya'll to ever forget it," C-loc said before sending them back to their rooms to play.

It never occurred to the boys that this would be the last time they would see their fathers alive, but they would always remember the words that they were told.

CHAPTER 1

Brandon felt sad as he neared his brother CJ's house, because this was the day that he and his grams were moving from the infamous Femosa Way in Homewood to the notorious Bedford Avenue in the Hill District and they would be leaving his bro behind.

He thought about all the good times that he and CJ had together, and he knew that he was going to miss his bro a lot. When he reached the house, he walked up the steps and knocked on the door, sighing to himself as he waited for an answer.

"Who is it?" CJ's mom, Ms. Robinson, asked from behind the closed door. Homewood was so violent that nobody answered their door by peeping through the peephole, because they never knew if the barrel of a gun would be what they saw.

"It's Brandon, Ma. Is CJ there?"

Keisha opened the door and let him in. "How you doing?" she asked while leading him into the living room where CJ was asleep on the couch.

"I'm doing aiight," he replied, sitting down on the love seat across from the couch where CJ was sleeping.

Every time Keisha saw Brandon, she had to shake her head at how much he resembled his father. "How about Grams?" she asked. She and Grams hadn't been talking lately. *Who the hell is she to try and take my son*, she thought to herself.

"She's fine, too, now that we moving to the Hill," Brandon replied interrupting her thoughts.

"I didn't know that was today," she said as if she were surprised, when in fact she refused to let CJ move with them. Her main reason was so she could continue to collect her welfare checks. She also didn't want to believe in her head that she was an unfit mother. "Well, I guess that's why he been moping around all week," she said before going upstairs to her room.

When she was gone CJ sat up on the couch, shaking his head. "Finally," he said low enough so she wouldn't hear him and come back downstairs with her bullshit.

"Come on, bro, she ain't that bad," Brandon said laughing.

"You don't have to live with her" CJ replied, thinking about how she always nagged him. "So what's cracking, cuz?" he said throwing up a Crip sign with a smile on his face.

Brandon just laughed at him, knowing how badly he wanted to be a Crip like their dads were. He, on the other hand, just wanted to be a big-time drug dealer, and if he became a Crip in the process then it was cool with him.

They were complete opposites even though they considered themselves brothers. Brandon was more of a smooth-type person, always calm but ready to get down if he had to. On the other hand, CJ was a hot head and he stayed in some type of trouble. Whether it was fighting or cursing out a teacher in school, CJ was always the culprit.

Shaking these thoughts from his mind, he got back to the reason why he came to get CJ. "You act like you don't know what today is."

"Ya'll moving today, right?" CJ asked with sadness in his voice.

"You acting like it's the end of the world."

"Whatever, nigga." The truth was that to him it was like the end of the world, and he didn't know what he would do without his bro and Grams.

They both were silent for a while, engrossed in their own thoughts, neither of them wanting to part ways. After a few moments of silence, CJ spoke up. "I know ya'll need help packing some of them boxes," he said getting up from the couch.

"Yeah, come on before Grams come looking for us. Any-way, she want to see you before we leave," Brandon said leaving the house with his bro close behind.

They headed to Brandon's house, which was only a block away. This gave them a little time to talk about the plans they had made ever since hearing about the lifestyles their fathers had lived.

"So what you going to do while I'm gone?" Brandon asked with a serious look on his face.

"Ain't nothing going to change my dreams of becoming the *biiggeest* drug-dealing, gang-banging nigga in the 'burg," CJ replied with determination in his voice.

Both of them had dreams of becoming big-time drug dealers just like their dads. The only problem was the OGs in their neighborhood respected their fathers so much that they refused to let them in the game.

Their fathers had reached certified OG Crip status before they were killed in a drive-by shooting, supposedly over some drug money. They were never given the specifics of the murders, but they vowed to find out who killed them and get revenge.

The last time that they saw their fathers alive they were only six years old. It had been ten years, but they remembered the day and the words their fathers said to them as if it were yesterday. They had been arguing, as brothers always do, when their fathers came into the house and caught them. After chastising them for fighting, they asked the same thing they always did whenever they caught the two boys arguing: "Are you your brother's keeper?" Ever since then, they never argued and they always treated one another as though they were actual brothers, even though they didn't have the same blood running through their veins.

Brandon's mom died while giving birth to him, so when his dad died, he was left in the care of his grams.

Their fathers had been real close, both of them being raised under the same roof by Brandon's grandmother. She took Brandon's father in when he was only ten because his mother was addicted to crack cocaine and had no interest in taking care of her son. Grams couldn't stand seeing CJ's dad living as though he were homeless—going from house to house, not eating and wearing the same clothes for weeks at a time—so she adopted him.

Because of this closeness, Grams treated CJ as though he were her own. Another reason for this was that CJ's mother fell apart when his father died. CJ's father was the backbone of the family, and when he was alive she didn't have to lift a finger. But once he died, she was clueless. Luckily, Grams was there to pick up the pieces.

Most of the time CJ was at Gram's house, and she made sure he was always clothed and fed while his mother ran the streets as if she were still a teenager. She even tried to persuade his mom to let him move to the Hill with her and Brandon, but his mom refused, not wanting to give up her welfare checks or to be looked upon as an unfit mother.

When they reached Brandon's house, Grams was at the front door to greet them. "Look at what the cat done drug in," she said smiling.

"How you doing, Grams?" CJ asked her."

"I'm fine. I just wish your mother would have let you move to the Hill with us.""At least you tried," CJ said with sadness in his voice. He wished he were moving with them. They were all he had, and he knew that without them in his life, things would be rough.

"Lord knows I tried," Grams replied while staring off into space. She knew from all her years of living in Homewood that it was not a good place to raise a child. To make things even more difficult, both of her boys were coming up on their seventeenth birthdays and, although they were good kids, she would not be able to keep them away from the street life if that's what they chose.

"What else do we have to move?" Brandon asked, interrupting her thoughts.

"Just move them last few boxes sitting in the living room," she told them before going upstairs to make sure she left nothing behind.

"Let's get these boxes in this truck," CJ said as he picked one up and headed outside.

Brandon picked up another one and followed, neither one of them saying a word as they worked. It didn't take long to finish since Grams had already had the heavy furniture delivered to their new home.

Once the last box was in the truck, Grams came down the steps and gave CJ a goodbye hug with tears in her eyes. She hated to leave one of her boys behind, but she couldn't stand to live in Homewood any longer. There were too many murders and robberies and she just didn't feel safe.

"It's cool, Grams," CJ said, fighting back tears of his own.

"Just make sure you call me if you need anything. Your mom has the number."

"Aiight, Grams, I'll call," he assured her before breaking their embrace.

After giving him one last hug, she went to sit in the truck, giving the boys a chance to say their goodbyes before parting.

For a long moment all they could do was stare at each other and shake their heads, neither wanting to be the first to speak up. "

"So this is it," CJ said breaking the silence.

"This is it," Brandon replied as he hugged him.

"Homie, I'm a-miss you, bro," CJ said with tears streaming down his face.

"We still going to keep in touch. Anyway, I'm only moving to the Hill, not to another state," Brandon told him, trying to make it seem as though everything was all right, when, in fact, he had a strong feeling that life would separate them and send them in different directions.

"Just don't forget about me," CJ said breaking their embrace. He felt the same as his brother, and he knew there was no guarantee that he would even see his bro again.

As they stepped apart, Grams started the truck up to let Brandon know it was time for them to leave.

"Time to roll, bro," Brandon said as he hugged CJ one last time before turning to leave. He walked to the truck with his head sadly hanging. Before he could open the door, CJ called his name. "What's up?" he asked as he turned to take one last look at his bro.

"Am I my brother's keeper?" CJ asked smiling, just as he did when his pops asked him that on that deadly day ten years before.

"Yes, I am," Brandon replied before getting into the truck with Grams. He threw up a peace sign as he and Grams pulled off in search of a new beginning.

If he only knew what his future had in store for him . . . if he could only read into the future . . . he would have begged Grams to turn the truck around. Moving to the Hill would not keep him out of the streets. As a matter of fact, they would pull him in deeper than he could ever imagine. But he could not predict the future or change it. All he could do was sit back and take in the scenery of his old neighborhood as it passed by.

He looked out of the window at the dilapidated buildings and empty lots, as well as the drug dealers and gangstas on the block doing what they do best and sighed, hoping in his heart that he would not only *be* like them, but that he would be *better* than them.

He felt that being a drug dealer was the greatest thing in the world. What he didn't know and couldn't prepare himself for in any way, was the flipside of the game—going to jail or getting killed. And like so many teens with their drug dealer ambitions, he would have to learn the hard way.

After about five minutes of watching the scenery, he dozed off, wondering what laid in wait for him in the Hill District.

CHAPTER 2

"Wake up, Brandon," Grams said as they pulled up to their new house at 1802 Bedford Avenue.

He woke up and looked around. From what he could see, the neighborhood didn't look much different from the dirty trash-ridden streets of Homewood. The houses were a little newer looking, but from the trash littering the street and the crowded corner you could see that it was still the ghetto.

There was a mixed group of older and younger guys hanging on the corner not too far from the house, and he could tell by the red bandanas they all wore that they were Bloods.

There was also a group of girls standing beside the moving truck and paying them close attention as they checked out the scenery.

"Let's get out and have a look at our new house," Grams said exiting the truck. She was happy to be away from Homewood, and the pride that she felt from moving her grandson to this new place showed on her face.

Brandon got out of the truck and walked around to where Grams was standing on the curb. He had a feeling that someone was staring at him so hard they were burning holes in the back of his head. This caused him to look towards the corner, and he noticed a few of the young Bloods walking up the street.

He didn't know what to expect as he walked through the crowd of females in front of his house. Grams was oblivious as to what was about to go down. Trouble was the last thing she expected in this new neighborhood.

Halfway to the door, one of the females in the crowd spoke up. "He look good," she whispered loud enough for him to hear.

This was something he already knew, standing at five foot eight, light skinned with hazel eyes and three-sixty waves in his head, enough to make the females seasick. To top it off, he had a body that was immaculate for a boy his age; he was cut up like a bag of dope.

He looked at the girl who made the comment and was blinded by her good looks. As soon as he was about to say something to her, one of the young boys from the corner spoke up.

"Keep it moving, pretty boy," a short, stocky, dark-skinned kid with braids told him.

"Who the fuck you talking to?" Brandon asked with anger in his voice. He hated being called a pretty boy and he had punished many kids in his old neighborhood for making this same mistake.

"Who else I'm a-be talking to? You the only bitch-ass pretty boy I see standing out here."

Brandon was heated and was ready to explode, but before he could react, Grams intervened.

"Brandon, what is you out here doing?" she said grabbing him by his shirt and pulling him into the house.

Brandon mean-mugged the kid all the way into the house. He was pissed that the kid had even tried his nuts, and he knew that he would have problems with him in the near future.

"You should be happy that she saved you. Next time won't be no talking, just brawling," the kid screamed from outside.

"Whatever, nigga," Brandon replied wishing Grams would let him go so he could tear into the taunting boy's ass.

Seeing Brandon getting into trouble made her frustrated and Grams started to wonder if she made the right decision by moving. "What's the matter with you?" she asked giving him a serious look.

"Ain't nothing wrong with me, Grams. Anyway, he started it," he explained trying to defend himself. He could tell by the look in her eyes that she was really mad at him, but even though he hated to get her upset, he wasn't going to let anybody play him for a sucker.

"Look, Brandon, our whole reason for moving was to get away from trouble, not get into it." She could tell by the way he just stared at her that what she was saying went right in one ear and out of the other. *This boy is so stubborn*, she thought to herself.

Brandon knew that Grams would go on and on to get her point across, and even if she was wrong, she was right, so he just gave in. "I understand, Grams," he said in a defeated tone.

"Just go upstairs and cool off while I move some of the boxes into the house. When you're done cooling off, come help me with the rest," she told him before heading outside to the moving truck.

After she left, he went upstairs to do as he was told, going first to the bathroom and throwing some cold water on his face to cool down a bit. He knew that this ritual would work because he had done it many times before when he had been pushed to the limit.

Once he finished in the bathroom, he began to check all the bedrooms. Their beds and dressers had already been delivered and set up. He had to admit to himself that this house was a lot better than their old one—it was just the neighborhood that he didn't like. He knew that he would have to prove to everyone that he wasn't a punk before he could get respect. He also knew that one of the ways he could gain respect would be to fight the stocky kid that antagonized him. In fact, he was anticipating a fight with the kid soon.

After going through his room, he went into Grams' room, which faced the street. He stood by the window and, after scanning the block for a minute or two, his eyes landed on the stocky kid. He was standing on the corner with three other kids, all of whom had been in front of his house earlier when he almost got into the fight.

They were all standing around a tall black dude with long braids in his hair. This guy had on all black with a red flag, a bandana, hanging out of his back pocket on the right side.

Brandon watched them intently, wondering what they were up to when a car pulled up and parked at the curb, answering his question. He knew exactly what was happening, and he watched as the organized transaction went down.

The stocky kid walked up to the car and began to talk to the driver. After a few seconds of conversation, he turned around and put up three fingers.

One of the other kids nodded before going to their stash spot to retrieve something. Whatever he picked up he gave to one of the other kids who took it to the driver of the car. After receiving the package, the driver pulled away.

The stocky kid went over to the older guy with braids and handed him what looked like money. The other kid must have been the lookout, because he was scanning the block while the transaction was going down.

Brandon sat in the window and watched the scene play out a few more times before going to help Grams move the rest of the boxes into the house.

"About time," Grams said lugging a box into the house as he came out. She hoped that he was done cutting up because she didn't want to have to keep going through the same talks with him over and over again.

"My bad, Grams. I was just cooling off like you told me, and I checked out the house a little bit," he said before helping her move what was left of the boxes.

It took them a while to unload all that was on the truck. When they finished, it was getting dark outside and the neighborhood was bustling with energy. The whole time they were unloading boxes, he was catching glances from the stocky kid on the corner, and he could feel the tension in the air.

"Finally," Grams said with a yawn once the last box was in the house. "I'm going upstairs to lay down. Anyway, I got to take the moving truck back to the U-haul place first thing in the morning," she said before heading up the steps.

"I'm right behind you," Brandon said following her. He went to his room and began to unpack his clothes so he could throw on something a little heavier to fight the cold breeze blowing in from the river.

After unpacking, he took out a black hoodie with blue letters on it that read *Homewood* and put it on before heading outside to see what was cracking in this new neighborhood. On the way out, he stopped at Grams' door to let her know his plans.

"Grams," he whispered into her room, not knowing if she had already fallen asleep or not.

"What's wrong, baby?" she answered. By the sound of her groggy voice, he could tell that he had awaken her.

"I'm about to go outside and sit on the porch for a while," he told her hoping she wouldn't make a big deal of it because of the trouble he had nearly gotten into earlier.

She wanted to tell him to stay in the house, but he was not a kid any more, and she knew that if worse came to worse, he could handle himself. "Just be careful, baby," she said before letting out a sigh. Now that he was nearly seventeen, she worried about him all the time, and she prayed that the streets wouldn't get hold of him and swallow him up.

"I'll be careful," he assured her before going down the steps. The truth was, he hoped that he could settle his problem with the stocky kid so he didn't have to worry about it anymore. Before he could make it out the door, Grams called his name and he stopped in his tracks. 'What up, Grams?" He hoped she hadn't changed her mind about his going out.

"Don't stray too far from the house." She didn't know much about the Hill District, and she didn't want anything bad to happen to her grandson. She felt that the closer he stayed to the house, the better.

"I'll be right out front," he said before going out the door. Once outside, he sat down and began to check out the scenery. *Damn, it's live over here*, he said to himself. When he looked across the street, he noticed the girl who gave him the compliment earlier. He licked his lips at her beauty, wondering if she had a boyfriend.

While he was admiring her good looks, she glanced in his direction and noticed that he was staring at her. She turned to her girls and said something that caused them all to start giggling.

Brandon thought the joke was on him, so he waved them off and focused his attention elsewhere. That's when he noticed the kid on the corner watching him with hate in his eyes. He didn't want to get into any more trouble for the day, so he looked back at the girl, only to see her walking in his direction. That made him smile from ear to ear, but he quickly put on his thug persona. "What you want?" he asked as she approached him.

"Damn, why you acting so mean?" she asked. Her hands were on her thick hips while she smiled to show her perfect white teeth and juicy lips.

"I seen you over there laughing at me with your little hood-rat friends."

"First of all, my friends are not hood rats, and we wasn't making fun of you."

"What was ya'll laughing at then?" He really wasn't mad at all, and he didn't care if they were laughing at him. He was just trying to get to know her and possibly make her his.

"We was actually laughing at how cute you look sitting over here trying to look tough . . . ."

All Brandon heard was that she thought he was cute. "So you think I'm cute?" he asked her.

"Don't get your head all big," she said laughing.

That caused him to laugh, easing the tension between them.

"So, cutie, what's your name?" she asked. His good looks had her blushing and her heart began to beat faster every time he spoke.

"My name is Brandon," he said, stunned by her beauty. He was like a deer caught in the headlights of a car. "What's your name?" he asked her once he regained his composure.

"My name is Quiana, but all my friends call me Ki-Ki. Being as though you ain't all that cute, you could just call me Quiana," she said, joking with him.

"Whatever, Ki-Ki." He already felt that he was in the friend category and soon would be in the boyfriend category. "So where your boyfriend at?" he asked her.

"Where your girl at?" she asked flipping the question on him. She knew that he must have a girlfriend back in his old neighborhood, because he just looked too damn sexy to not have one.

"I don't have a girl right now, but I was hoping you could fill that position," Brandon said running his game. He could tell by the way she looked at him that she was feeling him, even if she didn't want to admit it just yet.

"What if I already have a boyfriend?" she asked trying to play hard to get with him. She didn't want to give in to his good looks and nice personality on the very first day she met him.

"Do you?" he asked, hoping that she was free to be his.

"Maybe I do," she said playing with him.

He smiled at her response and the cockiness that he inherited from his father shined through in his words. "We'll tell him to kick rocks because he has been replaced."

"I'm a-stop playing with you because I do like you. I don't have a boyfriend. I'm not really looking for one right now, but we can be friends," she told him.

"Why don't you want a boyfriend?" he asked feeling rejected. He knew that he couldn't just be friends with her because her beauty had him in a headlock.

"I'm trying to focus on school right now," she explained. "A boyfriend would just get in the way."

"I understand," he told her. He did understand—in fact, he was feeling her even more because she had goals and was focused on her future. Anyway, he could tell that she was feeling him and he knew that she would open up to him in due time.

"So, Brandon, where did you move here from?"

He answered by pointing to his Homewood hoodie.

"Oh, my God!" she said as she looked at the words. The whole time they were speaking, she hadn't realized what he was wearing. If she had noticed, she would have told him to take it off.

He saw the expression on her face and wondered what her problem was. "What's wrong?" he asked her.

"You shouldn't be wearing that around here."

"I'm not worried about nothing. I can hold my own," he said, ready for whatever trouble came his way. As soon as the words were out of his mouth, he noticed the stocky kid walking his way.

Ki-Ki noticed him, too, and she knew that there was going to be a problem. 'That's just Bay Boe. He thinks that he is so fly because he be hustling, but everybody knows he be getting played."

Brandon didn't know a person who hustled that didn't make money. What she was saying sounded bogus to him. "How do you know he be getting played?" he asked.

"He barely keeps money in his pocket and what he do make he spends on weed and clothes." As he got closer, Ki-Ki began to get worried for Brandon's safety. "You should just go in the house."

Brandon didn't want to seem like a punk, so he stood his ground as Bay Boe walked up.

"What's up, Pretty Boy?" Bay Boe asked, standing in front of Brandon and Ki-Ki.

"My name ain't Pretty Boy!" Brandon said as he got to his feet. Before he could stand all the way up, Bay Boe punched him in his mouth.

"What now?" he said holding his hands in the air as if he already won the fight. Little did he know that he was far from wining, if he ultimately won at all.

Brandon shook the punch off and put up his hands, ready to prove that he wasn't a bitch. Bay Boe threw another punch, but Brandon slipped it and hit Bay Boe with a hook. The punch caught Bay Boe off guard and he stumbled backwards. After catching his balance, he rushed Brandon, catching a two piece to the face before slamming him to the ground.

It was then that Ki-Ki jumped into the fight and tried to break it up by pulling Bay Boe off of Brandon. This gave Brandon the chance to get back on his feet and he caught Bay Boe with another jab. Before Bay Boe could respond, the older guy with the braids who Brandon had seen posted on the corner earlier that day broke up the fight.

"You always making shit hot," he told Bay Boe. Brandon could see the anger in his eyes and could tell by the way he looked at Bay Boe that he wasn't someone to mess with.

"Fuck that, nigga!" Bay Boe said wanting to finish the fight.

"Fuck you!" Brandon replied ready for round two.

"Just go play the corner with the rest of them niggas," the older guy said before letting go of Bay Boe.

Bay Boe did exactly as he was told, which showed Brandon that the guy was definitely running things.

Once Bay Boe got back to the corner, he started arguing with his homies for not helping him, even though he already knew the reason why. They didn't want to be cut off from hustling by the guy with the braids because of Bay Boe's hot head.

As soon as Bay Boe was gone, the guy with the braids introduced himself. "What's up, li'l Ike? My name is Eight Ball," he said sticking his hand out for Brandon to dap up. Hill niggas said "Ike" in memory of their dead homie, Ikey Dog.

Brandon just looked at him. He didn't trust him enough to shake his hand after the altercation that he just had.

Seeing his resistance made Eight Ball laugh before he explained himself to calm Brandon's paranoia. "Look, li'l Ike, the only reason I'm even talking to you is because I liked the way you held your own fighting Bay Boe. Now you can be paranoid if you want. I won't blame you because paranoia is the key to survival. On the other hand, I'm trying to get to know you and show you how things go around here. So, what's your name?" he asked sticking his hand out once again.

This time he replied, even though he still didn't fully trust Eight. "My name is Brandon," he said dapping him up.

"That wasn't hard, was it?" Eight said smiling.

"Not at all," Brandon replied relaxing a little bit.

"I see you got your Homewood hoodie on."

"This is where I'm from," Brandon replied with pride.

"Well, look, this is a Blood set and you can't be wearing that around here. I'm not telling you this to try and scare you. I'm trying to keep you from getting into another fight. Anyway, sometimes it ain't about where you *from*, it's where you *at* that counts the most...feel me?

"I feel you," said Brandon understanding where he was coming from.

Eight liked Brandon's style, and he knew that he would have to catch him at another time to holler at him about getting on his team. "I'm a-go play this block and hopefully we will rap a little later," Eight said before he walked to the corner.

The whole time Eight was talking, Ki-Ki was quiet. She didn't trust Eight too much, so when he was gone she spoke up. "I don't think you should be messing with him," she warned Brandon.

"Why not?" Brandon shrugged his shoulders. "He seem cool to me."

"He seem cool, but he be getting into a lot of trouble. Also, he be manipulating all the kids around here to sell his drugs for him."

At the sound of selling drugs, he definitely didn't want to hear the shit she was saying. "Whatever," he replied. He hated it when people tried to tell him what to do as if he were a kid or something.

"You don't have to get an attitude. I was just telling you so you could be careful. If you don't want to listen, then that's on you."

"Why you so worried about me anyway?"

"Because I think that you're a good person, and I don't want to see you get caught up in no bullshit around here."

"Thanks, but I can handle my own," Brandon said as he got up to go into the house.

"All I'm saying is be careful, because even though it looks nice around here, bad things do happen to good people."

"Just because I'm young don't mean I'm dumb, Ki-Ki. I know what it's like here in these streets, and I can hold my own. So don't worry about me." He went into the house, slamming the door in her face and leaving her standing on the porch with sadness in her eyes.

Once in the house, Brandon went upstairs to check on Grams and to let her know he was in for the night. "Grams," he whispered into her room. She didn't reply, but he could hear her light breathing, so he let her sleep and went to his own room to lay out his clothes for the next day.

He knew that he would have to get into another fight when he started school because the issue between he and Bay Boe was far from over, or at least that was what he thought. He decided that it would be best to just try and avoid him for now.

He was in the tenth grade which meant he would be going to Brashear High School, where the atmosphere was fueled by gang violence. He knew about Brashear from playing their team in basketball, and he knew that people from Hazelwood and Beltzhoover, which were Crip neighborhoods, went there with those from the Hill, which was Blood.

Since he was neither, he figured that he would be able to get his last two months of tenth grade out of the way without getting into trouble. The only problem he would have was Bay Boe, and he had no fear about handling that situation. "I wish we could have stayed in Homewood," he sighed.

Pushing his thoughts of Homewood to the back of his mind, he began to take out his clothes for the next day. His attire would consist of blue and gray Bo Jacksons, blue jeans, a white tee and a Georgetown Hoyas fitted hat. Lastly he pulled out the Cuban link that his dad left him and put it on top of his neatly folded clothes.

He undressed and laid back on his bed with his brother CJ on his mind. They had been through a lot together over the years, and he reminisced about the good times. *I'm going to call him tomorrow*, he thought to himself before drifting off to sleep.

CHAPTER 3

"**B**randon! Brandon!" Grams screamed over his dying body. He had at least two bullet holes and he was leaking blood everywhere.

Brandon looked into Grams' eyes and tried to say "I'm sorry," but the words wouldn't come out.

Grams began to shake him as if to keep him from falling into a never-ending dream, but he couldn't fight it. "Wake up, Brandon! Wake up!" she screamed once more, hoping that her voice could bring him back to her.

Suddenly he was back in the room sweating profusely, grabbing his chest to check for bullet holes.

"Boy, what's wrong with you?" Grams asked fearing that he was having a heart attack or something.

"I'm good, Grams," he replied realizing that it was nothing more than a bad dream.

After seeing that he was all right, she snapped on him. "Boy, you scared me half to death. What's wrong with you?"

"I just had a bad dream," he said while trying to remember what the dream was about.

"Go get yourself together, so you can come with me to take the moving truck back." She gave him a worried look as she left the room.

When she was gone, he got up and went into the bathroom. He hopped straight into the shower and enjoyed the hot water as it relaxed his body and mind. Once again he tried to remember what the dream was about, but he got nothing.

After a nice long shower, he brushed his teeth before going back to his room to get dressed. He threw on his dad's chain and his fresh outfit and went downstairs to wait for Grams.

After a short while, Grams came down the steps dressed and ready to go. "You ready?" she asked him.

"What about breakfast?" He felt like his stomach was touching his ribs.

"We can get something on the way there," she said as she ushered him out of the house.

Once outside he saw a whole different crowd posted on the corner, and he figured that they must switch up shifts. The kid who he had the altercation with was nowhere to be seen, and he guessed that he and the rest of the boys must be in school. It was only eleven o'clock and school didn't let out for another three and a half hours.

He couldn't wait until school let out so he could apologize to Ki-Ki for slamming the door in her face. This was the only thing on his mind as Grams drove to take the truck back. They stopped at McDonalds so they could fill their stomachs, and shortly after that they were at the U-haul place. After dropping the truck off, they headed back into town on a PAT transit bus, and Brandon thought about Ki-Ki the whole way.

*   *   *   *   *

Meanwhile, on the other side of town, CJ sat in the house thinking about what he was going to do now that his brother was gone. He had just gotten home from school and was about to start his homework when his mom walked in with her new boyfriend.

"Baby, you so crazy," she said giving her boyfriend a long kiss as if her son wasn't in the room. When she did notice CJ sitting on the couch, she smiled at him. "What you doing in here?" she asked him as though it wasn't his house as well.

"I was trying to do my homework before ya'll interrupted me," said CJ giving her a disgusted look.

"I don't know why you got an attitude with me for, but I know you better fix it," Keisha said going upstairs with all the bags of clothes that Blue got her from the mall.

"What you doing, li'l cuz?" his mom's boyfriend asked once she was gone. His name was Blue and he was an old friend of his pops.

The fact that he was messing with his mom made CJ upset because he felt Blue was disrespecting his dad's memory, but there was nothing he could do about it, so he kept his opinions to himself.

"You hungry, li'l cuz?" Blue asked after seeing that he wasn't going to answer his first question. He knew that his girl wasn't going to cook any time soon, and if he didn't look out the li'l nigga would go starving.

Food was something CJ couldn't turn down. Without Grams in his life, food would be scarce. "Hell, yeah, I'm hungry," he replied hearing his stomach growling at the thought of food.

Blue pulled out a knot and pealed off a twenty. "Go grab us something from Simi's," he said. He handed CJ the money and put the rest back in his pocket.

CJ eyed the knot as Blue put it away. "Damn, cuz, where you get all that dough from?"

"Don't worry about my money. Just go get us some wings," Blue said smiling at his interest in money. The face that CJ made when he saw the knot reminded him of his old head C-loc—CJ's pops—and for a second it brought back memories of better times.

Blue knew that he was wrong for messing with CJ's mom, but he just couldn't help himself. She was his weak spot and he had a crush on her ever since the day CJ's dad introduced him to her. C-loc didn't have a clue that he was feeling his girl, but Blue knew that as long as he was alive, he didn't have a chance with Keisha.

As soon as his old head C-loc was killed and was no longer in the picture, Blue began to put his thing down. The thing was, she looked at him as her man's flunky, so she played him time and time again throughout the years. Just recently, though, she decided to give him some play. The truth was, she was no longer the hot young thing that she used to be, and niggas weren't tricking on her like they used to. She was in luck though, because Blue was right there to pick up the slack. In fact, he was more than happy to take care of her.

Blue felt guilty about what happened to C-loc, and he felt that he should be looking out for CJ. Since he had always had a crush on Keisha, everything worked out for the best.

*   *   *   *   *

While CJ was on his way to the store, he began to re-evaluate his thoughts of Blue. *Maybe he ain't so bad after all*, he thought to himself. Most of his mom's boyfriends didn't give a damn if he went starving, just as long as they got what they wanted from his mom.

When he arrived at the store, he walked through the crowd of people who were out front, dapping a few of them on his way inside. After placing his order, he sat down in one of the booths and waited for his food.

"What up with you, CJ?" one of his friends, whose name was Arab, said as he entered the store.

"Just picking up some food for me and the nigga Blue," CJ said dapping him up.

"What's up with the nigga Blue? I heard he fucking with your mom now."

"Yeah, they mess around." CJ really did not want to get into the specifics of his mom's personal life.

"I wonder what your pops would think if he was still alive." Arab hadn't known C-loc when he was alive because he was the same age as CJ, but he heard many stories about the things he did, and he knew he wasn't someone to be fucked with.

"I was thinking the same thing when they first started fucking around, but to each his own, you know."

"Here go your food, sir," the cashier said interrupting their conversation.

"About time." He grabbed his food, dapped Arab up and headed home to feed his growling stomach.

"Damn, li'l cuz, what took you so long?" Blue said grabbing the food from his hand as soon as CJ walked through the door.

"My fault, cuz. I was talking to Arab."

"That nigga ain't nothing but trouble," Blue said walking into the kitchen to get some hot sauce for his wings.

CJ ignored him because he knew that he was just as much trouble as anybody else.

After hooking his food up, Blue sat down in the living room on the couch across from CJ. "So you be hustling, li'l cuz?" he asked between bites of food.

"I wish," CJ said going hard on his food. He was so hungry that he didn't even look up from his food.

"Why you want to be a hustler?" Blue asked.

"Go look in the refrigerator and then ask me that question."

The words he spoke and the look in his eyes said everything. Blue grew up in a similar situation and he understood everything.

As they ate the rest of their meal in silence, Blue tried to contemplate whether or not he would turn CJ on to the stick-up game so he could put some money in his pockets. Although he was messing with his deceased friend's woman, he still had some type of respect for him, and he knew the high standards he had for his son. He could even remember the words C-loc used to speak as if it were yesterday: "I don't want my son growing up to be like me . . . . this life ain't for him." With that being said, he didn't want to get CJ caught up in the life.

Halfway through his meal, he looked up and studied CJ. He saw a young nigga with a hunger inside of him that would pull him to the streets no matter what people did to try and keep him away; he was just a product of his environment.

It was then that he decided to take him on a robbery, and he hoped that he was prepared for what lay ahead.

CHAPTER 4

While Brandon was sitting on his front porch waiting for school to let out, Eight Ball came walking up from the corner to greet him.

"What up, Ike? What you doing out here?" he asked.

"Just checking out the scenery, trying to get used to the neighborhood."

"I hear you, Ike. I see you got that iced-out chain on. You must have been killing the block in Homewood."

"Nah, I ain't never hustled," Brandon said smiling.

"So where you get that chain from? What you be robbing niggas?" Eight asked him.

"My dad left me this chain when he died."

"I bet people always ask you if you slanging when they see you with that chain on."

"Yeah, I get that a lot," Brandon replied as he looked down at his necklace.

"So how old are you?" Eight asked. He guessed him to be at least eighteen.

"I'm only sixteen."

"Damn, Ike, I thought you was a little older than that."

Brandon knew that he was big for his age, and everybody he met thought he was older than sixteen. "So what's up with you?" He knew that Eight didn't just approach him to ask his age.

"Look, I'm not going to beat around the bush. I liked the way you handled your business last night, and I feel that you are a thorough young nigga. Now it ain't hard to tell that I got things on smash, and I want to know if you would like to hustle for me."

Nobody in the neighborhood hustled like Eight, which was the reason why he stayed out of jail. He never touched anything; instead, he used all the young homies to move his drugs for him. Even though he hustled this way, he still made a lot of money since he only paid his workers a small amount of what he made.

Before Brandon could reply to his proposition, the school bus pulled up.

"Oowheee," Bay Boe hollered as he stepped from the bus. This was the Blood call.

"Oowheee," Eight hollered back signaling for all his homies to come to him. "I'll get at you later, Ike," Eight said before leading his squad to the corner.

Brandon and Bay Boe had a staring match, but after seeing that he wasn't going to have any immediate problems, Brandon turned his attention back to the school bus just in time to see Ki-Ki get off.

She saw that Brandon was searching the crowd and figured he was looking for her, so she headed in the opposite direction when she got off the bus, not really wanting to talk to him after the previous night.

Brandon chased after her. "Yo, Ki-Ki, I need to rap to you."

"What you want?" She turned around to face him. Even though she was a little mad at him for slamming the door in her face, she really did like him and he had been all she could think about while she was in school today.

He caught up with her on the corner of Cliff Street and Cassett and immediately began to apologize. "Ki-Ki, I'm really sorry about last night."

She just stared at him, and when she didn't respond he continued, "I really dig you and I hope you forgive me for acting the way I did last night. I just hate when people try to tell me what to do as if I'm not able to take care of myself. That's why I snapped out." He ended his plea for forgiveness and hoped that she felt where he was coming from.

She still had her mean look on, but for real she was feeling him just as much as he was feeling her. The more she looked at him, the harder it was to keep up her front and this made her smile.

"What you smiling about?"

"You look all cute standing there trying to explain yourself," she giggled.

"So do you accept my apology?"

"Yes, I accept your apology, and even though we just met, I'm feeling you a lot and I really want us to be friends. I apologize for talking to you like you was a kid. So do you forgive me?"

Before he could reply, he heard someone calling his name from the top of the hill. When he turned around, he saw Eight Ball trying to get his attention.

"What is he calling you for?" asked Ki-Ki.

"Earlier he told me that he wanted me to be on his team."

"Well, we can't be talking then," she said matter of factly.

"Why you say that?" He looked back at Eight, who was impatiently waiting at the top of the hill.

"I don't mess with drug dealers or gang bangers," she said before walking away.

He wanted to chase after her, but didn't want to keep Eight waiting any longer, so he just shook his head and walked up the hill.

"Damn, Ike, you ain't hear me calling you?"

"Yeah, I heard you, but I was trying to holler at Ki-Ki."

"Forget about her. I got something way more important," Eight said as he led him to the corner.

When they walked up, he and Bay Boe began to mean-mug each other. If Eight hadn't been there, they would have definitely begun fighting again.

Bay Boe pointed at Brandon and said, "I know you ain't going to let this crab-ass nigga get money with us."

"First of all he ain't no crab, and secondly don't be trying to question what I'm doing," Eight replied getting fed up with his troublesome ass. It seemed like every day there was some bullshit going on because of Bay Boe.

Before things could get more heated, Brandon's grand-mother began to call for him. "I got to go see what she want," he said not wanting to be a part of their argument.

"That's right, nigga, you saved by the bell. Run home to your grams, you little momma's boy," Bay Boe said taunting him as he left.

Brandon didn't want to get into another altercation now that he was so close to getting in the game, so he ignored Bay Boe and kept moving.

After he left, Eight began to scold Bay Boe. "Nigga, why you always starting trouble with everybody?"

"I ain't fucking with no crab, Ike," he replied not trying to hear what Eight had to say. Crab was a disrespectful term for Crip.

"He ain't no crab and, anyway, I don't care what you say. The little nigga is going to be down with us so get used to it," Eight said before he walked across the street to the corner store.

Bay Boe was mad at Eight for recruiting Brandon, but he knew that Eight's word was final. "Maybe he aiight," he said to himself as he approached a customer.

The rest of his homies were quiet, but they were thinking the same thing as him.

"As long as he ain't no crab, I'm okay with him fucking with us," his homie Snype said breaking the silence.

"What about ya'll?" Bay Boe asked the rest of his homies, wondering how they felt about the situation. Everybody agreed that as long as he wasn't a crab, then he was cool.

"I guess he in then," Bay Boe said hoping that he and his homies weren't making a mistake by letting an off-brand nigga into their circle. *Only time will tell,* he thought to himself.

Brandon didn't know, but their decision would be the beginning of a whole new life for him.

CHAPTER 5

"What's cracking, cuz?" Blue said sitting on the couch next to CJ.

It had been two weeks since Brandon moved to the Hill District, and ever since he left, it felt like things were moving in slow motion. CJ hadn't been to school in about four days because Brandon was no longer around to wake him up every morning, and his mom and Blue didn't even try to get him up at all.

As he sat there on the couch, he made a promise to himself to get back on his education, because he knew that he might need it to get out of the hood. That is, if his dreams of becoming a big-time drug dealer didn't come true.

"You want to make a quick run with me?" Blue asked, interrupting his thoughts.

"Where to?" he asked not really wanting to go anywhere with Blue, who he was still feeling mad at for not getting him up for school.

"Don't worry about where we are going. Do you want to come or not?"

He thought long and hard, and he realized that he didn't have anything else to do. Anyway, he wanted to ride in Blue's Lexus. "Yeah, I'll ride with you."

"Come on then," Blue said heading outside.

They both hopped in his all-blue Lexus that was sitting on chromed out twenties. CJ laid back while Blue turned up the music and hit the gas.

"So you going to tell me where we going?"

"Just relax and enjoy the ride," Blue said, turning music up louder to block out his questions.

CJ got the message, and he kept quiet as they rode on to an unknown destination. After about a half hour of driving, they pulled up and parked on Sheffield Street in Manchester, which was on the North Side of Pittsburgh. CJ had never been to the North Side before, so he was not aware that they were in enemy territory.

Manchester niggas claimed OG and they didn't get along with Crips. If he had paid attention to the scenery, he would have seen that all of the niggas they passed were sporting all black with black bandanas in their pockets and on their heads.

"I'll be right back," Blue said grabbing his gun from under the seat before getting out of the car.

Seeing the gun made CJ tense up and he began to take a better look at his surroundings. He didn't see anybody around the place where the car was parked, so he relaxed a little.

About fifteen minutes later, CJ began to grow impatient. He looked in the rear view mirror and, to his surprise, Blue was running to the car with his gun in one hand and a bag in the other. *What the fuck*, he said to himself, wondering what or who Blue was running from.

Blue hopped in the car, breathing like he just got done running a marathon.

CJ looked at the bag sitting in Blue's lap and saw that it was full of clothes. "What's going on?" he asked in a panicked voice.

"Calm down," Blue told him. He was trying to stick the key in the ignition and look in the rear view mirror at the same time.

"What you mean, calm down?" CJ asked watching him fumble with the car keys. If anything, he was the one that needed to calm down.

After about thirty seconds of trying, Blue finally got the key into the ignition. "Thank God," he said.

As soon as the car started, CJ heard the sound of guns going off, and when he looked back, he saw two dudes about half a block away running down the street in their boxers. Both of the guys had their guns pointed at Blue's car, and they were letting off round after round.

"Why the fuck is they shooting at us!"

"Just get down," Blue said throwing the car in drive and fleeing the scene unscathed.

CJ sat in silence as they left the North Side, trying to figure out what he had just gotten in to.

Blue sat silent as well, but his silence was for a different reason. He didn't want to celebrate their escape before they were actually out of harm's way. It wasn't until they were halfway back to Homewood, crossing the Highland Park bridge, that Blue started laughing.

"What the fuck is so funny?" CJ asked looking at him as if he were crazy.

"You ain't see them bitch-ass niggas in their boxers?" Blue replied, laughing even harder.

"You're fucking crazy." CJ began to picture the two guys running down the street in their boxers and began to laugh as well. When he regained his composure, he asked Blue what happened.

"I'm a-tell you, but you have to keep this shit between me and you. Meaning don't tell your mom or anyone else," Blue said giving him a serious look as they pulled up in front of CJ's house.

"I ain't going to say nothing," CJ assured him eager to know what happened.

Blue looked him in the eyes and saw that he could trust him not to say anything, so he came out with it. "Them niggas that was chasing the car tried to buy some work off of me. Instead of selling it to them, being as though I didn't have it, I just robbed them."

Blue looked him in the eyes once again to see how he felt about the situation. He didn't see any fear or regrets in CJ's eyes, so he continued on. "There's two types of people in this world—the takers and the ones who get took, and as you can see, I'm a taker," he said letting him know what he was now involved in.

"So how much money you get off them niggas?"

"Don't worry about it," he said, pulling a knot out of his pocket. He had robbed them for three thousand, five hundred dollars all together. He counted out five hundred dollars and gave it to CJ for riding with him. "If you keep your mouth shut, then the next time I will let you in on the action."

Looking at the money in his hand made him think about his brother. He wished like hell that he was there with him so they could get money together. He also began thinking that if he could do a couple more robberies with Blue, he would be able to fulfill his dreams of becoming a big-time hustler.

"Come on, cuz, let's go in the house before your moms come out here complaining and shit," Blue said interrupting his thoughts.

As soon as they walked through the door, his mom was bitching. "Where the fuck ya'll been? I know you ain't have my son around none of your funky-ass hoes." All she really wanted to know was that her man wasn't cheating on her. Even if Blue told her that he got her son shot at, she wouldn't care, just as long as there weren't any females involved.

"Come on, Keisha, you need to stop your nagging bullshit. I only took him for a ride around the hood," he said giving CJ a look that read, don't say shit.

"Don't be having my son in no bullshit, Blue," she said as if she actually cared. "I know how you are, and I don't want my son getting hurt."

"Relax, baby," Blue said giving her a kiss before leading her up the stairs to give her what she really wanted—some dick.

Once they were gone, CJ pulled out the money he made and began to count it over and over again. He prayed that Blue would take him on another robbery soon, so he could save up enough money to get in the dope game.

After about ten minutes of fantasizing about his promising future, he heard the sound of his mother moaning. He sat back on the couch and sighed, wishing he was somewhere else. It was like this all the time with his moms, just different faces. That's one of the reasons he needed to get his money up and get his own spot as soon as possible.

He just wished his brother was still around so they could blow up together. After counting his money one last time, he laid back and wondered what his bro was up to. *Damn, I got to call that nigga*, he said to himself before drifting off to sleep.

*   *   *   *   *

Blue laid back on the bed waiting for Keisha to come out of the bathroom. He took a hit of his blunt and looked at his watch. *Damn, what's taking her so long*, he asked himself, anticipating a shot of that bomb-ass pussy that Keisha had.

As soon as he looked up from his watch, she came walking into the bedroom with some red high-heeled fuck-me-pumps and a red negligee to match. She was always a dime, but when she dressed up for him on that freaky shit, she was a twenty in his eyes.

"So, you ready for this pussy?" she asked crawling onto the bed as if she was a feline, purring and all.

"You already know I'm always ready, baby."

"Say no more then," she said pulling his boxers down and wrapping her juicy lips around his dick. "Mmmm, daddy, your dick tastes so good."

She was a cold freak and Blue loved every second of the bomb head that she gave him. She could look in his eyes and see that she had him sprung off of her, which is exactly how she wanted it.

When his dick was rock hard standing at attention, he told her to stop and turned her on her back so he could taste her pussy. She was dripping and he caught himself moaning at how good her pussy tasted.

"You like the way it taste, daddy?"

"Hell, yeah, mami," he said in between licks. She was grinding her pussy against his face, and he was licking up every drop of her pussy juice.

"I want you to fuck me now, daddy," Keisha said feeling her pussy throbbing in need of his hard dick.

"Be patient, mami," he said, turning her over on to her stomach.

"Oh my God, daddy," she said knowing what was about to come.

"Damn, I love your nasty ass."

She hollered as he ran his tongue down her ass crack while finger fucking her pussy at the same time.

"Whose pussy is this?" he asked while tonguing her down, licking up every drop of the juices that ran down to her ass.

"This pussy is all yours, daddy. Now fuck me!" she demanded.

Blue could hear the urgency in her voice. He lifted her ass in the air, sliding his thick dick into her pussy from behind. "Is this what you want, mami?"

"Yes, daddy," she replied throwing her pussy back at him, meeting him thrust for thrust as a juicy orgasm began to build up in her body. "Please don't stop, daddy!" she screamed loving how his dick felt inside of her. No one had ever fucked her like Blue, and she was kind of mad that she played all those years.

"Turn your sexy ass around," Blue said helping her onto her back and sliding his dick inside of her hot wet pussy.

"Oh my God, daddy, I can feel it in my stomach!" she screamed out.

This boosted Blue's ego and he began to pound her pussy harder and faster. Keisha wrapped her legs around Blue and tried to match his drive, but it was just too much.

"Damn, daddy, beat this pussy up!" she screamed feeling herself about to orgasm once again. "Come with me this time, daddy?" she asked, but he was far from busting a nut of his own.

"This is just the beginning," he told her knowing that he had at least another half hour of loving in him.

"I'm coming, daddy! Don't move!" she screamed shaking from head to toe. It felt like a tsunami rushing from her pussy, gushing all over Blue's dick.

Blue got up from on top of her and laid down on his back. "You know what I want."

Her riding game was on point, and this was how he always loved to end their bomb-ass sex sessions.

She slid her soaking wet pussy down on top of his long black dick. "You love this pussy, don't you, daddy?" she said riding him nice and slow. She loved riding him because it put her in charge and she could work it however she wanted. She used her pussy muscles to grip his dick as she milked it for that precious fluid he had inside of it. "Come for me, daddy."

He grabbed her ass cheeks and began to pound his dick deeper into her pretty little pussy. "Make daddy come," he said trying his best to beat down her pussy walls. "Oh, my God, you got some fire-ass pussy," he said feeling himself about to burst.

She could feel his dick throbbing inside of her and she knew it was almost time. "Please come in me, daddy," she said speeding up her pace, riding his dick like a straight pro.

He couldn't hold back any longer, so he grabbed her ass and pounded his dick in her pussy as hard as he could, bursting deep inside of her.

The force with which he came pushed her over the edge and she came with him. "Damn, that was good," she said laying on his stomach until she could gain her composure.

"Did you like it, mami?"

"Hell, yeah, daddy," she replied getting up to go into the bathroom to wash off. When she was done, she came back into the bedroom with a smile on her face. "So was that pussy good to you?" she asked him.

"Your pussy is always good to me."

"I ain't talking about *this* pussy. I'm talking about that trifling-ass hoe that you had my son around." Her smile turned into a frown to let him know that she wasn't playing any games.

"Keisha, I told you we wasn't over no hoe's crib."

"So where did you take him?" she asked with her hands on her hip and a serious look in her eyes.

"I just took him to go handle some business."

"What business did you and my son have to handle?"

"Just some business," he said getting out of bed with his dick out.

The sight of him naked kind of threw her off, but she wasn't giving in easily. "Blue, I don't want my son getting killed in them streets like his father did."

"What are you trying to say, Keisha?" Blue asked feeling offended by what she said.

"I'm just saying that I don't want nothing to happen to my son."

Blue knew exactly what she was trying to insinuate, and he didn't want to hear a word of it. He went to the bathroom to hop in the shower.

Keisha had heard rumors about Blue and CJ's dad and she knew that she was wrong for messing with Blue, but it was too hard to try to do things on her own, so she just bit her tongue and went along with the program. Anyway, even if she did say something, it wouldn't bring C-loc back.

CHAPTER 6

Today was Brandon's first day at Brashear High School, and he was rushing to get dressed so he wouldn't miss the bus. He had another bad dream about getting shot and, once again, he couldn't remember exactly what the dream was about. *Fuck it*, he said to himself while putting on his outfit for the day.

After getting dressed, he looked at the clock and noticed that he only had ten minutes left before he had to be at the bus stop. He put on his iced-out Cuban link to top off his outfit and looked in the mirror. He nodded his head in approval and left his room. Before leaving the house, he stopped at Grams' room to let her know that he was going out and also to ask her for some lunch money.

"Grams," he whispered hoping that she hadn't gone back to sleep after waking him up.

"What you want now?"

"Can I get some lunch money?" he asked even though he already knew the answer.

"You better eat them school lunches like everybody else. Money don't grow on trees, and we damn sure ain't rich."

"Aiight, Grams," he replied before heading down the steps. *I wish I was hustling*, he thought, thinking of Eight Ball's proposition. Then he thought about Bay Boe, and he knew that he was not going to be able to hustle with him because of the never-ending problems they seemed to have with each other.

He had avoided Bay Boe all weekend and he dreaded having to go to the same school as him. In his heart he felt like their problems were not solved, and he was prepared for another fight if that was what he wanted.

Shaking his problems with Bay Boe from his head, he brushed his clothes off and stepped out the door. He walked to the bus stop, which was right across the street from his house. Ki-ki, who was still not talking to him, was there. He also saw Bay Boe standing off to the side with his homies.

He tried not to pay much attention to Bay Boe, hoping to avoid another altercation, but it really didn't seem like Bay Boe wanted to start anything, so he walked over to Ki-Ki.

"What's up, sexy?" he asked hoping she'd give him some play.

She replied by rolling her eyes at him and acting as if he wasn't standing right in front of her.

Before he could say something about her attitude, Bay Boe tapped him on the shoulder from behind. "What's up?" he asked throwing up his hands ready for round two.

"I come in peace, Ike," Bay Boe said letting him know that he wasn't looking for any problems. "I know that you can hold your own," he added letting Brandon know that he earned respect.

"No doubt," Brandon replied cautiously. The last time he let Bay Boe get too close it cost him a blow to the face.

"Yo, Ike, me and my homies had a talk and we decided that we going to let you get down with us."

"What makes you think I want to get down with ya'll?"

"If you like getting money, then you should get with us. Anyway, Eight already told us that he want you on the squad and it's not a good idea go against what he say."

"Well, I definitely want to make some money, and if I can do that with ya'll, then I'm down."

"I'm happy to hear that because I can tell by the way you carry yourself that you are an aiight nigga," Bay Boe said before dapping him up.

"I feel the same about you," Brandon said returning his embrace.

"Now that we got that out of the way, I need to ask you a serious question."

"Speak what's on your mind."

"How come you wasn't banging out Homewood?"

Brandon explained how his dad was an OG Crip, and being as everybody had respect for him, they tried to keep him out of the street life.

"I feel you, homie, but just to let you know, we be going at it with the Crips in school, and we need to know who you going to be riding with."

"If ya'll ride for me, I will ride for ya'll. Anyway, it's like Eight told me last night . . . ."

"What's that?" Bay Boe asked.

"It ain't always about *where* you from, sometimes it's about where you *at*," he said smiling at his new homie.

"No question, Ike," Bay Boe replied. He then went over to his squad and let them know that they had a new homie.

After Bay Boe waked away, Brandon turned his attention back to Ki-Ki. "So you still made at me?" he asked hoping that she had a change of attitude.

"So you a Blood now?" she asked giving him an evil look.

"You eavesdropping now?"

"Quit beating around the bush, Brandon, and answer my question."

"Look, I'm just trying to get some money," he said trying to let her know what his true motives were.

"For you not to be a kid, you are so naïve," she told him.

"What you mean by that?" he asked feeling insulted by her comment.

"You honestly think they going to let you get money with them if you ain't no Blood," she said laughing at him.

"If you was listening, then you would know that I don't gang bang," he said trying to defend his actions.

"Like I said, you are so naïve." She stepped close to the curb at the sight of the bus coming down the street.

The bus pulled up at the curb and everybody filed on, going to the seats that they usually sat in. He got on last, not wanting to sit in anybody else's seat and possibly cause more problems that he had already gotten into.

After getting on the bus, he saw an open seat next to Ki-Ki, so he walked back to where she was sitting. "You don't mind if I sit with you?" he asked her.

"It's a free country," she replied while staring out the window.

Just as he was about to sit down, Bay Boe called to him from the back of the bus. "Come sit with us," he said pointing to an empty seat next to him.

"Nah, man, I'm cool right here," he said looking at Ki-Ki to see if she wanted him to stay. She rolled her eyes and waved him off to let him know that he wasn't welcome, so he went to the back of the bus with Bay Boe and his homies.

After he sat down, Bay Boe began to introduce him to everybody. "As ya'll know, this is the new homie, Brandon. This is LK," he said pointing to a skinny brown-skinned guy.

"What up with you, Ike," LK said dapping him up.

"This is my man, Snyper," Bay Boe said pointing to another light brown-skinned guy who was the same weight as LK only a little taller.

"What up?" Snype said dapping him up.

"This is Bundy," he said pointing to a brown-skinned guy with braids. He also introduced him to Mr. Boo, who was a dark-skinned dude with a low hair cut. They all gave him a warm welcome and he could feel the immediate love that they had for him.

"If something go down in school, we going to be the ones to have your back," Bay Boe told him.

"That's what's up," Brandon replied glad to be a part of their family.

After being introduced to everybody, he turned his attention back to Ki-Ki. She was a beautiful girl, light skinned with long hair and pretty hazel eyes. She stood about five foot five and had a banging body. He could only imagine what she would look like in the years to come.

Bay Boe saw him staring at her and interrupted his thoughts by saying, "I see you got a thing for her."

"I'm definitely feeling her, but she got a fucked-up attitude."

"Don't take it personal. She act like that to everybody."

"Why?" Brandon asked. He was tired of her funky-ass attitude and he wanted to know what her problem was.

"Look, Ike, I'm a-tell you what's up, but don't let her know that I told you."

"Homie, I ain't going to say nothing. I just want to know what's up with her," he replied frustrated.

"Well, her older brother was a Blood and he got killed in a drive-by shooting at the age of fifteen. That's why she don't fuck with nobody who is gang affiliated," Bay Boe explained.

Hearing her story made Brandon feel her pain, and he wished that he could comfort her. He looked at her and shook his head at the thought of her loss. He understood why she didn't want him being involved with Bay Boe and Eight Ball. He sat in silence the rest of the way to school, wondering what he could say to her to make things right.

He knew that he would not cut ties with his new homies because he wanted a piece of the drug game. He just hoped that they could compromise and meet somewhere in the middle because he really liked her.

After thirty minutes of riding and thinking, the bus pulled up to his new school and Bay Boe tapped him on the shoulder to let him know they had arrived. They got off the bus and headed straight to the breakfast line where his homies treated him to whatever he wanted.

Bay Boe and his squad showed love to all the other Blood homies who went to school with them, and then they posted up at their usual spot by the lockers in the hallway.

Whenever someone would ask who Brandon was, Bay Boe would introduce him as his homie Pretty Boy, and he let everybody know that he was riding with them. Since Bay Boe's word was good as gold, everybody respected Brandon, who was now known to the world as Pretty Boy.

CHAPTER 7

CJ woke up and looked at the clock on the living room table. "Fuck," he said out loud noticing that he had missed the school bus once again. It was a few days after the robbery and Blue had yet to take him on another.

For that reason he had been holding onto his money, trying to figure out what his next move would be. He pulled out his small knot and began to count it, making sure that nothing was missing. After counting it twice, he was satisfied that every dollar was there. Right after he put his money back in his pocket, Blue came walking in to the room.

"Why you ain't in school?" he asked as if he didn't wake him up on purpose.

"Why ya'll ain't wake me up?" CJ asked him.

"I was sleep just like you. Anyway I got something more important for you to do that going to school."

"What can be more important than school?"

"I'll tell you on the way to breakfast," Blue said standing up.

At the sound of breakfast, CJ jumped up off the couch and followed Blue out to his car.

When they got in the car, Blue turned up the music and CJ laid back in his seat. He felt like a king in Blue's plushed-out Lexus and all eyes were on them as they cruised the streets of Homewood.

After about twenty minutes of riding, CJ glanced in Blue's direction and noticed that he was watching him out of the corner of his eyes.

"What's up?" CJ asked wondering why Blue was staring at him.

"Anybody ever tell you that you look like your pops?"

"I get that a lot," he replied smiling at the thought of having his pops' features. "Tell me about my dad?" he asked Blue hoping that he knew more than what Grams had told him over the years.

Blue had a thousand stories he could tell about his pops, but he felt that he should tell of the situation that led to his death. Or at least he would tell his version of the story.

"As you already know, your dad was a OG Crip in the hood. In fact, he put me down with the set back in the day. When he was alive, he had me robbing everything moving and if a nigga had a problem with us, then we dealt with them.

"We called him Crip Loc or C-loc and he taught me everything I know about the stick-up game. Well it was him and your friend Brandon's dad, who we called Loco. They were both older than me, so I was their young nigga and I soaked up game from them like a sponge.

"I pulled some good licks with them niggas, and I ain't talking about no little petty-ass robberies. I'm talking big money on a regular basis," Blue said thinking of the good old days.

"What was your biggest robbery when my dad was alive?"

"We hit a lot of good licks, but there was one right before he died that put us all on top. Although it was a lot of money, it came with a hell of a price to pay."

"What you talking about?" CJ asked, knowing that it had something to do with his dad getting killed. He could see that Blue didn't really want to keep on, but he had to hear the true reason for his pops getting murdered.

"There was this young blood nigga from Garfield named CK Black who was a big-time drug dealer. He was only seventeen, but he was getting some serious money and he had the cheapest coke in the city. Rumor was he had a brother who lived out California that flooded him with one hundred birds a month."

"Damn, that's a lot of coke," CJ said thinking about what he could do with a connect like that.

Blue continued on, "This was at a time when you could easily sell a bird for thirty grand in Pittsburgh, and he had them for twenty grand a pop, seventeen if you was copping ten or more. The only problem was he was only serving Bloods, so we couldn't get close to him on our own. But when your dad and Loco got wind of him, they decided to do their homework on the nigga so we could get him for all he had.

"So after a few months of watching him, we decided to hook up with this Blood from Garfield named B-braze. He use to put us on Blood niggas that was moving major work, so that was our way in. We got in touch with him ASAP and he assured us that he could hook up a meeting with the nigga."

"Hold up. If ya'll Crips, then why was ya'll best friends with a Blood?" CJ asked interrupting him.

"First of all, there ain't no discrimination when it comes to taking money. Secondly, B-braze grew up with your dad in Homewood before gangs came to Pittsburgh. He moved to Garfield and became a Blood later on down the line. Even after he became a Blood, your pops still kept in touch with him."

Hearing this made CJ think about Brandon and he knew that if his bro became a Bood and him a Crip, he would still love him. "I feel where you coming from," he said under-standing the situation.

"Like I was saying, B-braze hooked us up with CK Black. He introduced us as some East Hill Bloods, and everything was gravy. Now if we didn't have B-braze that shit would not have worked."

"Why not?"

"At the time, the Hill, East Hills, and Garfield had a thing going on called EastGarHill or E.G.H. and all CK Black would have had to do was make a call to find out if we were who we said we were. But being as though B-braze vouched for us, CK Black didn't question our credibility."

Blue paused once again to pull out a cigarette and after he fired it up he continued on with his story.

"So once CK Black seen that we were cool, we hooked up with him and did some business. It took about three months for him to let his guard down, but when he did we got him for forty birds of cocaine."

CJ couldn't believe what he was hearing, and he thought that Blue must have meant four birds and not forty. "You say ya'll robbed him for forty birds?" he asked in disbelief.

"Forty of them thangs and we got to keep our cop money," Blue replied taking a long drag from his Newport.

"So where all the money go?" CJ asked thinking in his head that, if it were true, he wouldn't be robbing niggas for chump change, in fact he should be paid!

"We underestimated the nigga," Blue said with anger in his voice. "We thought that since he was so young, he wouldn't even think about getting back at us, but we were wrong," he said thinking back on all the bloodshed that followed the robbery.

"That still don't explain where all the money went."

"I'm getting to that," he said waving CJ off so he could finish telling the story. "Like I was saying, we got the nigga for forty birds and we split them up evenly, ten apiece. Now we was always robbin' niggas for thirty to forty thousand and sometimes a little more, but this was forty keys. We was all amped up, selling the keys for the low-low to put the hood on. Also we was flossing all over the city. Jewelry and cars wasn't nothing to us . . . we were ghetto celebrities.

"We had two houses on the same street, one where we moved the work and the other where we stashed the money and drugs. About three months after the robbery, the police noticed some drug activity coming from the houses and they ran up in both of them.

"I had just scored with all of our money, so all the coke we had as well as a bunch of guns got grabbed in the raid. It was close to seventy birds, a hundred thousand and around thirty guns. We bought the keys off of our Crip connect on the North Side at twenty-five thousand a bird, so that hurt like hell.

"To be honest, we wasn't that stressed about our spot getting hit. At the time we was just happy that we had just left the spot to get something to eat. All in all we chalked the whole situation up to bad luck, and we felt like we could get everything back in due time."

"I can't believe ya'll lost all that shit," CJ said shaking his head.

"The whole situation was fucked up and so were we at the time. All we had left was these chains that we spent fifteen thousand apiece on and a few old school cars that we bought and tricked out."

"So what ya'll do with all the chains and cars?"

"Well I told you how we underestimated CK Black and when our spot got hit and our guns got grabbed, me and your dad sold our chains and some of our whips to buy some guns because shit was getting hectic in the hood."

"I know Brandon's dad must have sold his car, too, but what did he do with his chain?" CJ asked.

"It's the same chain your friend Brandon always be wearing. His dad never sold it because he still had a couple dollar stashed at his mom's house. Your dad would have had some money in the tuck as well, but your moms was spending money like it went out of style and he kept her in the latest."

CJ knew how his mom was and he could only imagine how much of his dad's money she went through.

"Anyway, like I was saying, cuz wasn't no bitch and all the while we were splurging, him and his niggas was riding on whoever they thought crossed him.

"In the midst of all this, B-braze bought a new Benz and this was at a time when niggas wasn't even *riding* in Benzes. This drew the attention of CK Black, letting him know that he had something to do with robbery."

"Hold on though," CJ said confused. "Wouldn't he have known anyway being as though B-braze introduced ya'll to him?"

"It wasn't like that because of the way we set it up. Me and your dad didn't go to meet him this day. It was just B-braze and Loco. When CK Black showed up, we robbed everybody making it look like we all took a loss. We even tried to convince him to give us some work for our loss, but he wasn't hearing it because he took a loss as well.

"When B-braze popped up with his Benz after he supposedly took a hundred and seventy thousand dollar loss, CK Black knew what it was."

"So what happened to B-braze?"

"They kidnapped his dumb ass and tortured him until he gave us up. Next thing we know, niggas was riding through the hood spraying shit up in search of us.

"But it wasn't like we was on some hoe shit, homie, we was riding to. If you ask anyone about your dad they will tell you that he was definitely a gansta. CK Black just had an advantage because it wasn't just him putting in work."

"Well, who was it then?" CJ asked.

"He had brought in some Bloods from California that nobody knew and they would come through in the same kinds of cars that niggas from the hood had. That's how they caught me, your dad and Loco slipping," he said pausing once again. This time he had tears in his eyes.

CJ saw the tears streaming down his face and he thought they were for his pops, but it was deeper than that. "So what happened?" he asked nudging Blue on.

Blue wiped his eyes and continued telling the story. "One day we were on Femosa waiting for one of the li'l locs to come back with a stolen car so we could put in some work. All of a sudden, we see this black Grand National on gold Daytons coming down the street at a slow pace.

"We didn't think nothing of it because one of the locs had a car just like it, so your dad and Loco walked to the car to holler at him while I stayed back a little. But when the car pulled up in front of us, a nigga hung out of the window with a AK-47. the nigga had a blue flag over his face and when we realized what was really gong on, it was too late. The nigga started shooting and your dad and Loco didn't have a chance.

"They were closer to the curb than I was, so I had time to take cover only catching a bullet in the stomach. The niggas let off at least on hundred rounds and I played dead until I hard them pulling off."

When Blue got finished telling his story, CJ sat in silence until they pulled up to the breakfast spot.

"You aiight, li'l cuz?" Blue asked seeing him in deep thought.

"I'm just thinking about my pops."

"I miss him like hell, too, but that's how the game go. You live fast, you die faster," Blue said trying to ease his own conscience.

"I feel you," CJ replied understanding that it was a cold game. What he didn't know was niggas like Blue were even colder.

"Come on, man, let's go grab some grub because I'm hungrier than a muthafucka," Blue said getting out of the car.

"You read my mind," CJ replied hearing his stomach growling.

While they were waiting on their food, CJ spoke up. "Is the nigga CK Black still alive?"

Blue didn't want to answer the question because he knew in his heart that he should have killed him years ago. He looked CJ in his eyes and thought about lying to him, but instead he told the truth. "He's still alive, but him and his squad is stronger than ever. You can't even get in his hood without him knowing. Also you never catch him out by himself anymore. The nigga never slips."

What Blue was saying sounded like a whole bunch of bullshit to CJ, but he didn't let him know what he was thinking. He just nodded his head to make Blue think that he felt where he was coming from. Now that he knew how his pops was killed, all he could think about was getting revenge.

Blue could see the wheels turning in his head and he knew that he should never have told him about his pops being killed. The thing was he felt guilty for the part he played in their murders and he felt better off telling him his version of what happened than someone else telling him the truth. "If the opportunity presents itself, I'm with you," he told CJ not wanting him to think that he was shady for not retaliating.

"I hear you," CJ replied as the waitress sat their food on the table.

They ate in silence, both of them engulfed in their own thoughts. When they were done eating, they paid the waitress and left the restaurant. After leaving the parking lot, CJ turned the music down so Blue could hear him. "So when you going to take me on another robbery?"

"You could roll with me tonight."

"How much is it for?" CJ asked hoping that it wasn't a petty-ass five hundred dollar robbery like the last one.

"It's going to be for something nice, but are you sure that you're ready for this life?"

"I'm definitely ready," CJ answered wanting to live up to his dad's name. Now that he knew his pops was a stick-up kid, he wanted to rob everything moving.

When they got back to CJ's house, he laid down on the couch and thought about CK Black. He wondered what the nigga who killed his pops looked like, and he prayed that one day he would be able to avenge his dad's name.

CHAPTER 8

Even though he didn't like the name at first, it began to grow on him. Anyway it didn't seem as if he had a choice in the matter, because everybody took the name and ran with it. Whenever he was walking the halls after class, somebody would walk up to him saying "What up, Pretty Boy?" and he never corrected them. He heard the name so much in the first three periods that he just became cool with it.

Halfway though the day, around fourth period, he was walking to his next class when he ran into Ki-Ki and a few of her friends. "What up, Ki-Ki?" he asked trying to get some conversation out of her.

"Don't you mean, what up, Blood?" she replied sarcas-tically. "Is it still Brandon or should I just call you Pretty Boy."

Before he could respond, one of her friends jumped into the conversations saying, "Oohhh, so you're the pretty boy that everybody is talking about," in her most flirtatious voice.

"The one and only," he said feeling his new name more than ever.

Ki-Ki rolled her eyes at him and tried to walk away, but this time he grabbed her by the arm.

"What's your problem?" he asked her.

"I told you before that I don't mess with gangbangers."

"I'm not in no gang," he said defending himself.

"You hang with them and they gave you a nickname. You one of them now."

He felt what she was saying, but he didn't look at it as a bad thing. Deep down inside he was cool with being in a gang. When he was living in Homewood, he was never allowed to become a Crip because of his dad's past. Now he was being given a chance to get money with the Bloods and he was looking forward to his future on the set.

"Brandon, are you even listening to me?" she said interrupting his thoughts.

"I hear you, but maybe this is what I want."

"Well I can't be associated with you then," she said walking off to class.

This time he let her go because he was tired of chasing her around. He heard the bell ring for class to start and he headed to his own class. On his way there, he ran into two Crips from Beltzhoover.

"What up, cuz?" they asked him looking for trouble.

"My name is Pretty Boy and I ain't your cuz," Pretty Boy said poking his chest out.

So you Pretty Boy from the Hill?" the Crip standing on his left asked him.

"Yeah, that's me," he replied ready for a fight. As soon as the words left his mouth both of the Crips began hitting him with a barrage of punches.

"Get him, cuz," the smaller of the two yelled as Pretty Boy began meeting them punch for punch.

It was then that the two Crips realized that they made a mistake by picking him to fuck with.

Pretty Boy grabbed the smaller Crip and slammed him to the ground. The other tried to pull him off of his friend, but it wasn't easy. When he finally pushed Pretty Boy to the side, they tried to pin him down, but he wasn't going out like a sucker. He began throwing all of the punches that he had in him. Tired of taking a beating, the Crips backed up and ran off to class before security began to make their rounds.

Pretty Boy got himself together and did the same. As soon as he entered the classroom, he was questioned by the teacher about his tardiness. "Why are you so late?" she asked while looking up at the clock on the wall.

"I couldn't find the class," he replied hoping she accepted his excuse and let him be.

"Since you are new, I will let you slide . . . but the next time I'm going to send you to detention, understand?"

"I understand," he said sitting down in one of the empty seats in the back of the class. After getting situated, he looked around to see if any of the Crips who jumped him were in the room. He didn't spot any of them, but he did see Bay Boe sitting two seats over.

Bay Boe had his head down on the desk trying to go to sleep when he heard someone calling his name. He picked his head up and looked around the room until he saw that it was Pretty Boy. "What's up, Ike?" he said low enough so the teacher wouldn't hear him.

"Some Crips tried to jump me in the hallway," Pretty Boy told him with anger in his voice.

"Is you serious?" Bay Boe asked.

"Yeah I'm serious. The two niggas couldn't do nothing with me though, so they ran off to class before the security came."

"As soon as class let out, we going to look for them. All you got to do is point them out and me and the homies will handle the rest."

I'm a-do more than just point them out, Pretty Boy thought to himself.

"If ya'll are going to continue to talk in my class, then ya'll can go to detention," the teacher said putting them on blast.

They were both quiet as if they weren't the ones who were talking.

"That's what I thought," the teacher said before turning back to the chalkboard to continue her lesson.

As soon as class let out, Pretty Boy and Bay Boe walked around gathering up their homies. When everybody was together, they headed to the cafeteria in search of the two Crips who jumped him.

Once in the lunchroom, they stood at the front entrance. "There they go right there," he said pointing in the direction of the two known Beltzhoover Crips.

Bay Boe recognized them as C-side and Baby Blue. "Them niggas tried to jump you?" he asked in shock knowing that the two niggas were cowards and they would have never tried him.

"Yeah, that's them."

"Let's go handle this," Bay Boe said leading his homies over to where the Crips were sitting. "What's poppin', Baby Blue?" he asked.

"Ain't nothing, Bay Boe," he replied with fear in his voice.

Everybody knew that Bay Boe was known for fighting and he rarely lost. "I hear ya'll tried to jump my homoe." It was more of a statement than a question.

"Come on, cuz. I would never disrespect you or any of your homies," said Baby Blue trying to stay clear of a beat down.

"What about him?" Bay Boe said pointing to Pretty Boy who was standing behind Baby Blue.

When he looked behind him, he knew that he was in trouble. "Cuz, I didn't know that he was your homie and if I did, that shit would have never went down."

Bay Boe was tired of the small talk so he punched Baby Blue in the mouth.

"Dam, cuz, what you hit me for?" he asked holding his hand to his bleeding mouth.

"Nigga, you know what it's for," Bay Boe said punching him again. This time he knocked him to the ground. "And that's for calling me cuz," he added standing over top of him.

Pretty Boy saw C-side trying to slip away and he hit him with a two piece, knocking him out cold. "That's for trying to jump me!" he screamed at C-side who was on the floor unconscious.

Bay Boe saw the crowd forming and he knew that security couldn't be too far behind, so he grabbed hold of Pretty Boy and led him out of the lunch room. They headed straight for the boy's bathroom where they decided to chill until shit cooled down.

"You see how I knocked that bitch-ass nigga out!" Pretty Boy said amped up.

"Yea, I seen you," Baby-boe replied laughing.

"I'm ready for whatever," Pretty Boy said shadow boxing in the mirror.

"Calm down, Mike Tyson. We got to kick it here until lunch is over so security don't be on us."

"I feel you," Pretty boy said relaxing. The last thing he wanted was to get busted by security and be suspended on his first day of school.

When the bell rang for lunch to be over, they left the bathroom and headed to their separate classes. About fifteen minutes after class started, security came in and began talking to the teacher in Pretty Boy's class.

He sat there in silence praying that they were not there for him. After a few seconds of talking to the teacher, they called him to the front of the class.

"Is this Brandon?" the security guard asked to make sure they had the right person.

"Yeah, that's him," the teacher replied.

"I need you to come to the principal's office with me," the guard told him.

"For what?" he asked as if he didn't already know.

"You'll find out when we get there."

Pretty Boy followed them to the principal's office in silence. When he got there, Bay Boe and the two Crips were already in the reception area.

"Damn, Blood, they told on you, too?" Bay Boe asked as he sat down.

"We didn't tell. It was somebody in the crowd who told," Baby Blue said trying to defend himself.

"Shut up, pussy! Ain't nobody tell you to talk!" Bay Boe said giving them the thousand-yard stare. This caused them both to remain silent for fear of receiving another ass whooping.

Acting as if the two Crips weren't even in the room, they began to converse about how much trouble they were in.

"So what they going to do?" Pretty Boy asked him. He wasn't trying to get suspended on his first day of school, because he knew that would really upset his grams.

"They probably going to give you a three-day suspension, but they going to kick me out," Bay Boe told him confirming Pretty Boy's fears. The last time he got suspended for fighting, the principal told him that he would send him to the Option Center if he fought again. The Option Center was a school for kids that messed up one too many times and he was definitely in that category.

The principal called them into his office one by one. Bay Boe got expelled. Pretty Boy received a three-day suspension. The two Crips were only given detention since they were not the aggressors in the fight.

The rest of the day passed by quickly, which was funny, because Branon would have rather it passed by slowly. The last thing he wanted to do was tell Grams he got suspended.

Throughout the day he ran into Ki-Ki and she ignored him every time he tried to speak to her. He wasn't pressed though because he had a bunch of other girls checking for him, and although they were not like her, he knew he had to move on to someone different.

When the bell rang for school to let out, he met up with Bay Boe and the rest of his homies in the hall and they headed to the bus together. Since Bay Boe was already expelled, he punched every Crip he saw in the mouth on his way out.

Pretty Boy just laughed the whole time at how wild Bay Boe was. He could see that Bay Boe was a thorough nigga and he knew that they would be tight from then on. When they boarded the bus, Pretty Boy went straight to the back with his homies. He didn't even glance in Ki-Ki's direction as he passed by her.

When he got to his seat, all of his homies gave him props for knocking C-side out and he felt like they were all family. He knew that he would ride for his new brothers no matter what and he would prove it every chance he got. The whole way back to the Hill, everybody talked about how brazy he and Bay Boe were, and he sat back and enjoyed their praise.

When they got to the Hill, all of them exited the bus and posted on the corner for a while before heading in their different directions. Pretty Boy dreaded telling his grams that he was suspended and he explained his dilemma to Bay Boe.

"If you don't want to get into trouble, then don't tell her," he replied matter of factly.

"Then if the school call and tell her, I'll really be in a bad situation," Pretty Boy replied.

"The school never calls and if you worried about where to go in the mornings, you could just come to my spot and kick it until school let out."

"What about your parents? What they going to say?"

"My mom don't give a fuck and my dad is in jail, so it's all good."

"I'm a-think about it," he replied not knowing for sure if he was going to take Bay Boe's advice.

"Well, the option is definitely there."

"No doubt," Pretty Boy replied dapping him up before heading home to face Grams. He just hoped she didn't sense anything wrong with him.

As soon as he walked in the house, she called him to the kitchen where she was cooking dinner.

"So how was your first day of school?" she asked him.

"It was cool," he replied not wanting to go into detail. "So what you cooking, Grams?" he asked quickly changing the subject.

"Chicken and French fries. If you hungry, go upstairs and wash your hands while I put you a plate together."

At the thought of food, his stomach began growling and he realized that he hadn't eaten since breakfast. He went upstairs and did as he was told so he could get his grub on. When he was done, he went back downstairs and sat at the table to eat.

After setting his plate in front of him, Grams sat across from him and watched him as he was eating.

He could tell that she had something on her mind. He just hoped it wasn't the suspension bothering her. "What up, Grams?" he asked breaking the silence.

"I'm just sitting here wondering if us moving to the Hill will give you a better chance at life."

"This was definitely a good move, so you don't have to worry about anything happening to me."

"I know that, but when I look at you I see so much of your father and I honestly don't want you to live the same life he did."

"Grams, just know that whatever road I choose, I will be careful. You have to understand that I am a man now and I have to make my own decisions in life."

It was then that she realized that her baby would be swallowed by the streets. She realized that it didn't matter whether she lived in Homewood or on the Hill, because it was all the ghetto. She just hoped that he didn't become a victim to the streets like his father had.

Just as quickly as it came to her mind, she shook it off. The thought of something happening to Brandon sent chills down her spine, and she knew that she would lose her mind if she lost him.

"I know you're a man and I will support you no matter what road you chose," she said letting him know that she had his back. "Just be careful and smart in your choices. Remember that the streets don't love nobody."

"I hear you, Grams," he said getting up to put his plate in the sink. He felt where she was coming from, but at the same time he wanted all the things that the game had to offer and he would worry about the consequences later.

After their conversation, Grams went upstairs to catch the rest of her soap operas, leaving him at the kitchen table to think about what she told him. He was thinking hard, trying to plan out his moves for the future, when the doorbell broke his concentration. He got up and went to the front door, looking through the peep hole first. He could see that it was Bay Boe on the other side so he opened it.

"What up, dog?" he asked letting him in the house.

"I'm just out here hugging the block. Is you coming out?"

"Hell, yeah. Just let me go tell my grams I'm rolling," he said running up the steps. He let his grams know what was up and all she said was to be careful. He then went to his room and took his chain off, then put on an all-black hoodie. When he was done, he went back downstairs and hit the block with Bay Boe.

They walked down to the corner where everybody was out hustling. Eight Ball was on the corner as well, and he greeted them as they walked up.

"What up, li'l Ikes?" he asked dapping them up.

"What up?" they both replied.

"It ain't nothing but money out here, and I know ya'll trying to get some."

"Hell, yeah," they both replied.

"Well the package is in the stash and you get ten dollars off of every hundred you make, same as always," he told Bay Boe.

"I got it, Ike," Bay Boe said looking out for any snaps, also known as customers.

"You sure you ready to get down with the squad," he said turning his attention to Pretty Boy.

"I'm one hundred and ten per cent sure."

"Well, Snype ain't out here and I need someone to play lookout. You get five dollars an hour so how much you make depends on how long we stay out here."

"I'm cool with that," he replied happy to be on the team.

"So what's your name again?" Eight asked him.

"Brandon . . . but everybody call me Pretty Boy now," he said with pride.

"Pretty Boy, huh. I like that name. It fits you," Eight told him.

The name had already grown on Pretty Boy and the fact that Eight liked the name made him like it even more.

They played the block all day and the rest of the squad didn't show up at all. This made Eight furious and when Bay Boe told him that they went on a hook-up with some hoe, he was heated even more. By doing this they violated one of the key rules of hustling—M.O.B. or Money Over Bitches.

It was about one in the morning when Eight Ball paid them, and before he left, he told them to be on the corner when school let out the next day.

When he was gone, Pretty Boy pulled out his money and began to count it. "I can't believe he paid me fifty dollars for playing lookout a couple hours."

Bay Boe was happy that his homie was cool with the arrangement and he smiled as he counted his money over and over.

"So how much did you make?" Pretty Boy asked him out of curiosity. He knew that it was a good day for Eight, but he didn't know how much money actually come through the block.

Bay Boe pulled out his money and counted out three hundred dollars. *Yeah, today was an aiight day*, he thought to himself.

"That's a lot of money for a few hours work," Pretty Boy said surprised.

It was a good day," he replied thinking of the days when he barely pulled in a hundred dollars.

"If we do this every day, we could really get paid," Pretty Boy said doing the math in his head.

What Pretty Boy didn't know was that Bay Boe had been saving his money for the past six months. Minus the clothes, weed, food and bills, he had at least twelve thousand in the stash. He was saving up so he could get his own crib outside of the hood, and he knew that he would get there soon if he continued to do what he was doing.

It was getting late and Pretty Boy knew that Grams was probably worried about him, so he told Bay Boe he would see him first thing in the morning.

"I'm a-just kick it out here a little while longer," Bay Boe told him.

"What could you possible do out here this late?"

"Probably grab some weed or something, so I'll see you tomorrow unless you trying to smoke."

"I'm good," Pretty Boy replied. He didn't smoke and he couldn't understand why Bay Boe would spend his money on it. Especially after risking his freedom to get it. "Just be safe out here," he said dapping him up and going home.

When he got in the house, he went straight to Grams' room to let her know he was home, but she was already asleep. From there he went to his room and began to get his clothes ready for the next day. He took out his black Rocawear jeans, a black t-shirt, all black Air Force Ones and a black and gold Pirate's fitted hat. He then pulled his money out of his pocket and began to count it again before putting it in an empty shoe box and sliding it under his bed. He knew that if he and Bay Boe saved their money, they might be able to get their own corner and then they could make some real money. With this on his mind, he laid back and drifted off to sleep, fading away into another one of his bad dreams....

CHAPTER 9

Grams was lying in bed when she heard the shots. "Oh, my God!" she said jumping out of bed and running to the front door. Something inside of her told her that it was Brandon who was in trouble and she felt that she needed to save him. She opened the door to see Brandon and his friend, Bay Boe lying on the ground bleeding.

Brandon's friends were standing over top of him, trying to console him by letting him know that help was on the way. Grams broke through the circle of people and fell down on top of her grandson's body, crying and screaming his name.

"Brandon don't die! Wake up!" she screamed while shaking him at the same time.

This woke him up from his dream, and once again he was clutching his chest and sweating profusely. His grandmother thought something was wrong with him and she ran to the bathroom to get a wet washcloth. When she came back, she put the rag on his head to cool him down.

"Are you aiight?" she asked concerned.

"I'm cool. I just had another bad dream."

"You starting to scare me with these dreams. I'm a-have to take you the doctors to see if something is wrong with you."

"I don't need to see no doctor. It was just a dream," he told her once again.

"Well, what was it about?"

"I can't remember," he said trying to bring it back to memory.

"Maybe it's a good thing that you don't remember it," she told him before going back to her room.

After she left, he went to the bathroom to get himself together. When he was done with his morning ritual, he went back to his room and put on the clothes that he put out the night before. Once he was fully dressed, he put his Cuban link on and looked at himself in the mirror. His attire was up to par, so he headed to Grams' room to let her know he was leaving.

"Aiight, Grams, I'm out. I'll see you when I get home from school."

"What you want to eat for dinner tonight, baby?" she asked him before he could leave.

"Same as yesterday," he told her as it was his favorite meal. He then left the house and went to the bus stop to meet up with Bay Boe.

When he got to the bus stop, he was greeted by all of his homies. They were treating him like he was family and he was feeling the same way. All he heard from them was, "What up, Ike?" and "What's poppin', Blood?" as they dapped him up. After saying what up to all of his homies, he pulled Bay Boe to the side and let him know that he had decided not to tell Grams about being suspended.

"Smart move, homie," he replied. "As soon as the bus come, we going to head back to my spot to kick it until school let out."

"Sound good to me."

After standing at the bus stop for a few minutes, Ki-Ki came walking up. She walked right past him without speaking and her attitude pissed him off. He walked up to her and tapped her on the shoulder to get her attention. She turned around and rolled her eyes at him as if he disgusted her, but before she could turn away he spoke up.

"Why you got to act all funny?" he asked trying to get to the bottom of their problem.

"I'm not acting funny. I already told you how I feel about you."

"Why can't you just give me a chance to be cool with you and be your friend or something?"

"Just so you can get me involved in your gang activities? Nah, I don't think so."

"I would never do anything to hurt you," Pretty Boy told her. Ever since he heard about her brother, he felt sympathy for her and he wanted to be her shoulder to lean on.

Ki-Ki wanted to believe him because she was feeling him. She wished that he wasn't in a gang, because then she would definitely open up to him. Her main reason for not wanting to get into a deep relationship with him was the chance he would get killed or go to jail. After losing hr brother to the streets, she felt that she couldn't stand to lose another loved one.

On the other hand, she thought that maybe she could change him once they were together. She really liked him and she knew that she should at least give him one chance.

Before she could explain how she truly felt, the bus came down the street.

"Ki-Ki, we really need to talk later when school lets out," he told her hoping that she would finally give him some play.

"Why can't you just talk to me now?" she asked as the bus pulled up to the curb.

"I got suspended for three days about the fight I had with C-side," he explained.

"Aiight then, Pretty Boy. I guess we will talk later."

"You don't have to call me that if you don't want to," he told her as she got on the bus.

"Why not?" she asked him.

"That's what the homies call me and I'm hoping me and you can be more than just that. Anyway, I like it when you call me Brandon."

"Aiight, Brandon," she said as the bus driver closed the door.

When the bus pulled off, they headed for Bay Boe's spot, which was around the corner from the bus stop on Roberts Street. Not wanting to be seen by his grams, they cut through Ralley Alley and entered his house through the back door.

Bay Boe's house was a pure example of the slums. It kind of reminded him of CJ's house back in Homewood. There were dishes stacked up in the sink and bags of garbage overflowing in the trash can.

"We going upstairs to my room," Bay Boe said signaling for Pretty Boy to follow him. When they got there, he pulled out a key to open the pad lock on the door.

"Why you got a lock on the door?" Pretty Boy asked wondering what he was trying to protect in the almost abandoned house.

"You'll see once we get inside," he replied while opening the door.

When the door opened, Pretty Boy was shocked at what he saw. The room was like a whole different world compared to the rest of the house. There were designer jeans, sneakers and fitted hats everywhere. Also there was a big stereo and a fifty-two inch television in the room.

"Damn, dog, where you get all this shit from?"

Bay Boe just laughed as he opened up his closet door, revealing a safe. Before he opened it, he paused and looked at Pretty Boy who was watching from behind. "You know I fuck with you, right?" he asked him.

"I know," Pretty Boy replied wondering what he was about to be shown.

"You got to swear you won't tell nobody about this," Bay Boe said seriously.

"On my dad's grave, I won't tell no one."

Bay Boe could tell that his word was good, so he opened up the safe. Inside there were two thirty-shot Glock forties and a bunch of money wrapped in rubber bands.

"Damn, dog, where you get all that dough from?" Pretty Boy asked surprised.

"I been saving up all my money from the last six months."

"So how much is it?"

"It's about twelve grand in there. I would have had more, but when I first started hustling for Eight, I was spending all my money on bullshit. Then one day I got tired of just splurging and I began to stack. That's why Eight fuck with me so much. He see my ambition and he know that I got goals."

"I'm not going to lie . . . I thought you were broke," Pretty Boy said thinking about what Ki-Ki told him.

"What made you think that?"

"Ki-Ki said you be getting played hustling for crumbs and shit."

This made Bay Boe laugh. He wondered why Pretty Boy believed Ki-Ki's bullshit.

"Why you laughing?" Pretty Boy asked looking at him as if he was losing his mind.

"It's funny to me how people think I'm broke. If they only knew . . . ," he said shaking his head.

"Well, seeing is believing," Pretty Boy told him looking at all the money in the safe.

"Just do the math. I make at least a hundred dollars a day and that's three stacks a month. At the least I spend a thousand a month, so in six months that's twelve thousand. I pay all the bills in this house, but that ain't shit because at the least I *make* a hundred dollars a day. Some days I pull in two or three hundred a day," he said after doing the math for Pretty Boy.

Thinking about all the money made the wheels turn in Pretty Boy's mind.

"What's on you mind, homie?" Bay Boe asked seeing him deep in thought.

"What if we had our own corner? Just think about all the money we could make."

"I hear you, but the situation we got is already working for us."

"I'm saying, though, you just made twelve grand in six months . . . so imagine what Eight made."

"Believe me I know, but he got the connect and he the one that came up with the idea of organizing shit."

"I feel like we only getting crumbs when we can be getting some real money. Maybe Eight could help us get started with our own situation."

"He ain't going to be trying to hear that, and without him where are we going to get some work from?"

"That's definitely something to think about," Pretty Boy said trying to think of someone he could holler at.

"And even if we do get a connect, what corner is we going to post up on? Because them niggas out there ain't going to let us set up shop on their corner."

"That's not the only corner on the Hill," Pretty Boy said knowing that they could find somewhere else to get money.

"I agree with you, but where is we going to get some coke from?"

"I don't know, but it can't be that hard to get some."

"Look, homie, I'll check into it, but for now we need to keep doing what we doing," Bay Boe said not wanting to mess up what they had going on with Eight until they had a sure way of getting money somewhere else.

He put the money back in the safe and took out a quarter of dro to roll up while they chilled.

"So what are we going to do until school let out?"

"I'm a-sit back, smoke this dro and play PlayStation. If you want some wreck then grab the other controller," Bay Boe said setting the game up. Before he pressed *Start*, he rolled up his dro and lit it. After taking a couple puffs, he passed the dutchee to Pretty Boy.

Pretty Boy just looked at the blunt, contemplating whether or not he was going to hit it since he never smoked weed before.

"You going to hit it or just look at it?"

Pretty Boy grabbed the blunt and put it to his lips. After taking a long drag, he started coughing up a lung and beating his chest like King Kong.

"You aiight?" Bay Boe asked patting him on the back.

"I'm good,' he said passing the dro back to him. He had tears in his eyes and his forehead was sweating, but once the effects from the dro kicked in, he relaxed. The high was great and he enjoyed the calm feeling.

Bay Boe took a few hits of the dutchee and passed it back to Pretty Boy. This time he grabbed it without thinking. He loved the high and he knew that he wouldn't stop smoking any time soon. They passed the blunt back and forth while playing the game, both of them focused on beating the other.

After an hour of playing, Pretty Boy put the controller down. "I'm finished," he said lying back on the couch with his eyes closed.

"I'm tired of whooping your ass anyway," Bay Boe said standing up to stretch his legs.

"So what we going to do now?" Pretty Boy asked feeling groggy from the bomb-ass dro.

"I don't know about you, but I'm about to check the block out."

"Damn, dog, you going to just leave me here by myself?"

"Nigga, I ain't the one ducking my grams. Now I said you could hide out here, but I'm not going to hide out with you."

"That's fucked up," he replied getting comfortable. He knew that he couldn't go out and risk getting seen by Grams.

"I'll be back in a few hours to check up on you," Bay Boe told him leaving the room.

After he left, Pretty Boy plugged the game back in and played *Madden* until he passed out.

Bay Boe left the house and headed to the corner to see what was popping. It was only nine in the morning so there weren't too many people out. Usually Eight would be out in the mornings smoking weed as he waited for school to let out, so he decided to ask someone if they had seen him.

He walked over to a group of OG homies and greeted them. "What it be like?" he asked dapping them all up.

"Why you ain't in school, li'l nigga?" one of them asked.

"School is for suckas. I'm trying to get some of this block money. Feel me?"

"I feel you," the OG whose name was Pimook replied. "Is you trying to work the block for me?"

"I didn't even know you got down like that on the hustling tip. Anyway you know I only fuck with Eight as far as getting money go," he said, showing his loyalty to Eight Ball.

"The only reason I'm asking you is because it's hot out here. Anyway Eight ain't going to be around for a while, so you might as well get down with me."

"What you talking about?" Bay Boe asked him.

"Eight Ball, Taco and Rude Boy went to a drive-by last night and got into a high-speed chase before they could put the work in. there was two AKs in the car and the car was stolen. Also they had been looking for Eight about a homicide he did a while back. I'm surprised you ain't see it in the news."

"That's fucked up," he said wondering what he would now do for money.

"It's definitely fucked up and I know you trying to get some money, so you might as well run this work off for me."

"I'll move it for you," Bay Boe said wanting to make some quick money before going to check on Pretty Boy.

Pimook told him where the stash was and he began his routine, running back and forth to cars for the next three hours. He was the only person out with work so the package was gone in no time.

He made one thousand, five hundred from which he only got seventy-five dollars. Pimook was a tight-ass nigga and he later told Pretty Boy that he didn't do enough to get paid ten dollars off every hundred he made.

"I'm out," he said after getting paid.

"Hold up, Ike. I still got some work in the crib if you trying to move it for me."

"A nigga can't hustle on an empty stomach, dig me?" he replied hearing his stomach growling.

"I hear you. Just make sure you come back when you're done."

Bay Boe didn't even reply as he walked away because he knew that he would never hustle for Pimook again after what he paid him. This made him think of the conversation he and Pretty Boy had about getting their own corner.

He was tired of making a bunch of money for everyone else and only getting crumbs. Even though he had a nice chunk of change in the stash, he knew that he could be making a lot more if he had his own work.

When he got to his house, he went straight to his room and found Pretty Boy asleep on the couch. "Wake the fuck up, nigga!" he screamed at the top of his lungs, scaring him half to death.

This made him jump up from the couch gasping for air while holding his chest as if he were having a heart attack.

"You aiight?" Bay Boe asked concerned.

It was hard for Pretty Boy to respond because he was trying to catch his breath. "I'm good," he replied once he regained his composure. "I was just having a fucked-up dream."

"It must have been some dream," Bay Boe said while opening his safe up. He took out one of the thirty-shot Glock forty's and put it on his hip.

"Where you going?" Pretty Boy asked him.

"To get something to eat. You coming, right?"

"Hell, yeah, I'm coming, nigga. I got the munchies like a muthafucka," he replied.

Bay Boe got on the phone and called a jitney, the ghetto taxi or hackney that charged a flat rate to take a person anywhere in the city.

"Service," the jitney driver asked after about five rings.

"I need a car to twelve Roberts Street, going downtown to Market Square," Bay Boe said into the phone.

"That's going to cost you seven dollars," the jitney driver told him.

"I got you," Bay Boe replied.

"Well, I'll be there in ten minutes," the jitney driver said before hanging up the phone.

"You want to take the other gun?" he asked Pretty Boy before closing up the safe.

Pretty Boy had never carried a gun before, but he knew that he would have to be strapped at all times if he was going to be in the streets. "Yeah, I'll take the gun," he answered.

Bay Boe handed him the other Glock. He also took out a thousand dollars just in case they saw something they wanted to buy.

Pretty Boy put the gun on his waist and covered up the protruding clip with his zip-up hoodie. Then they went downstairs to wait for the jitney to come.

While they were in the living room waiting on the jitney, Bay Boe was admiring his chain. "Yo, Ike, where you get that chain from?"

"This is the only thing my dad left behind when he got killed."

"That shit is iced out. It must be worth a couple stacks."

"Honestly, I don't know how much it cost. I just wear it in remembrance of my pops."

Before they could converse any further, the jitney driver was out front beeping the horn.

"We out," Bay Boe said going outside to get in the car with Pretty Boy following.

"Where in Market Square do ya'll want to be dropped off?" the driver asked as they got in the car.

"George Aikens," Bay Boe replied, sitting back in his seat as they pulled off.

After ten minutes of driving, they pulled up in front of the restaurant and Bay Boe paid the jitney before they got out of the car. Once in the restaurant, Bay Boe ordered fish sandwiches for both of them without even looking at the menu.

Since he'd never been to the restaurant, Pretty Boy went along with Bay Boe's choice. Once their orders were ready, they sat down to eat in a booth that was close to the window so they could watch the street.

"These fish sandwiches is banging," Pretty Boy said swallowing a big bite.

"That's why I brought you here," Bay Boe replied smiling.

They continued to eat in silence, only looking up to check their surroundings. Downtown Pittsburgh was known as Crip-Reject Central. Whenever Crips got run out of their hood, they would relocate downtown. Even though they were rejects, downtown was still a dangerous place for a Blood to be because there were so many of them in the area. Anyway, in the 'Burgh, the Crips outnumbered the Bloods ten to one. That's why Bay Boe and Pretty Boy had brought their Glocks.

"I see you done already," Bay Boe said, looking at him as he wiped his face and hands.

"Nigga, you murdered your plate, too," Pretty Boy said laughing.

Since they were both done, they got up from the booth and threw their garbage away before leaving the restaurant.

"Where we headed to now?" Pretty Boy asked, not wanting to go back to the house and be stuck inside for another two hours.

"We going to Honus Wagner so I can check these new Jordans out," Bay Boe said walking up the street.

Honus Wagner was one of the hot shoe stores in the 'Burgh and they were always up on the latest kicks. The store was only a block away, so they got there after only a few minutes walking.

When they entered the store, they went straight to the back where the new Jordans were on display. Once in the back, they noticed a Blood homie looking at the same Jordans that Bay Boe was interested in. They knew he was a Blood because he had a red bandana hanging out of his back right pocket.

"What's up, Ike?" Bay Boe said getting the homie's attention.

"What's up, Blood?" the homie said turning around to face him.

They gave each other the be-to-the-five handshake which was their set's handshake. After dapping Bay Boe up, he turned to Pretty Boy to do the same, but Bay Boe intervened.

"He just got down with the set, so he don't know the handshake yet," Bay Boe told him.

"I feel you," the Blood said before walking away to look at another pair of shoes. Since he didn't know them, he figured they were just some wannabes.

"There them Jordans go right there," Bay Boe said pointing out the shoes.

"They definitely nice," Pretty Boy said liking them.

They were so much into the shoes that they didn't hear the two Crips walk up behind them. "Fuck them dead-ass shoes," one of them said.

"What you say, Blood?" Bay Boe asked turning around to face the Crip.

"You heard me, slob," the Crip replied.

"Ain't no slob here, crab," Bay Boe answered lifting up his shirt to how the extended clip on his Glock.

When the Crip saw the gun, he immediately switched up his attitude. "My fault. It was misunderstanding," he said shaking in his kicks.

"Well I suggest ya'll get the fuck out of here before it be two dead crabs on our menu," Pretty Boy said lifting up his hoodie to show them that he was also strapped.

This caused both of the Crips to flee the store. The only reason they looked back was to make sure they were not being followed.

"I see ya'll li'l niggas ain't to be fucked with," the other Blood in the store said laughing at what just happened.

Hearing him laugh caused them to laugh as well.

"What set ya'll claim?" he asked them.

"The Hill District, 1800 Bedford Avenue Bloods," Bay Boe said with pride.

"I know one of ya'll OGs. He go by the name of Eight Ball."

"That's our old head. We use to hustle for him, but he got arrested last night," Bay Boe told the Blood.

"So ya'll family then."

"Without a doubt," Bay Boe told him.

"I like the way ya'll handled that little situation and I need some young niggas like ya'll on my team."

"What team you talking about?" Bay Boe asked him.

"Let me introduce myself. My name is CK Black and I'm reppin' that five trey Columbo Blood all day," he told them.

Bay Boe knew the name and, from what he had heard, CK Black was the hardest banging money getting blood in Pittsburgh.

"You're the CK Black from Garfield?" Bay Boe asked, not believing it was really him.

"The one and only."

"I thought you never went out by yourself because of all the enemies you have?"

"I'm here now and ain't nobody trying to get at me. But forget all that. Like I was saying, I like ya'll style and I would love to do business with ya'll. I heard you say ya'll was hustling for Eight, but do ya'll be getting real money?" he asked, knowing that they must be doing something because of the chain that Pretty Boy had on.

"We was running for Eight, but now that he locked up we down and out," Bay Boe told him.

"I'm not talking about running. I'm talking about real hustling as in moving weight."

"We was talking earlier about how we need a connect so we can lock down our own corner," Pretty Boy said joining the conversation.

"Here, take my number and once ya'll get ya'll money right give me a call," CK Black said jotting down his number on a piece of paper.

"What's the prices like?" Bay Boe asked him.

"Twenty thousand a key and I'll front ya'll whatever ya'll buy."

"Sound good to me." Bay Boe knew that they could get rich off of prices like that.

After their conversation, CK Black dapped both of them up and left the store.

"You don't know who that was?" Bay Boe asked Pretty Boy.

"Nah, I never heard of him."

"That was CK Black and he got the Columbo projects on lock. Also he put in more work than a twenty-four hour store."

"Well, I never heard of him, but it look like we found the connect we needed so bad."

"You right about that," Bay Boe said motioning for the clerk so he could buy himself and Pretty Boy a pair of the new Jordans.

After the clerk rang up their shoes, they left he store and headed for Fifth Avenue where all the courtesy jitneys were. They didn't run into any problems, which was all good since they now had serious moves to make.

It didn't take them long to flag down a jitney and they were back at Bay Boe's house in no time. After settling down in his room, they began to talk about their new situation.

"So how we going to do this?" Pretty Boy asked.

"How we going to do what?"

"You know I just started hustling, so I don't have no dough to pitch in on the work."

"Don't worry about it. From here on out we brothers and what's mine is yours. Anyway I can't do this by myself, so I need you to have my back." Bay Boe told him as he opened up his safe to replace the money he didn't spend and to take out what was left of the quarter of dro and two blunts.

Pretty Boy couldn't believe what he was hearing and he knew that Bay Boe was truly a real nigga by his actions. "It's funny how we only been knowing each other for a minute and you showing me all this love," Pretty Boy said surprised by his loyalty.

"Real recognizes real," Bay Boe told him. In his eyes this saying explained everything. Pretty Boy was down to ride for him one hundred per cent and it showed. He knew he could trust him, and he knew that he was a real nigga. He rolled up the last two blunts of dro and they spent the next couple of hours smoking and playing PlayStation as they waited for school to let out.

CHAPTER 10

When CJ woke up, Blue was sitting on the couch across from him smoking a blunt. "What time is it?" he asked Blue.

"It's six o'clock," Blue answered while trying to pass him the blunt he was smoking.

"I'm good," CJ said fanning the smoke from in front of his face

"More for me then," Blue said taking a long hit of the dutchee. "So you ready for the lick tonight?" he asked CJ giving him a hard look.

"I'm ready, but what do I got to do?"

"All you got to do is lay the bitch down and grab the dough. If the bitch move or resist in any type of way, then you let her have it."

"I don't have a gun to lay her down with."

"I got you," Blue said pulling an AK-47 from under the couch he was sitting on and handing it to him.

"What the fuck am I going to do with this?" he asked looking down at the big-ass gun in his hands.

"Hand it here, so I can show you how to use it."

CJ handed the gun over and Blue first showed him how to put one in the chamber by cocking it back, then showed him how to work the safety. "When you shoot it, brace yourself because you a little nigga and it got a lot of kick."

CJ was only a hundred pounds soaking wet with his timbs on. He stood five foot six, which was a few inches shorter than his brother Brandon. The only thing they had in common was their complexions and the three sixty waves on their heads. But, all in all, both of them were pretty boys.

"I got this," he said taking the gun back from Blue. Even though he never shot a gun before, CJ knew that if it came right down to it, he would put a bullet in a nigga at the drop of a dime, no hesitation.

"I got to go make a move," Blue said after CJ assured him that he could handle the gun.

"When you coming back?"

"Around nine o'clock...and make sure you dressed in that all black when I get back. Take this mask and these gloves also, because you going to need them," he said handing them to CJ and leaving.

When he was gone, CJ sat there staring at the gun in his hand, eager to put it to use, when his moms walked up behind him.

"What you doing with that gun?" she asked looking over his shoulder.

"Nothing," he said sliding it back under the couch. He was so caught up thinking about what he would do with the gun, that he didn't even hear her coming down the stairs.

"You better not be in them streets getting into trouble with Blue's crazy ass."

"I ain't getting into trouble. I just like to chill with him because he's cool."

"Who you think you talking to with that bullshit. I know what Blue does out there in them streets. You're just like your dad with your lying bullshit, and if you keep running around with Blue then you going to end up dead like your dad, too."

He hated when his mom tried to shit on his dad's memory, like he didn't take care of her when he was alive. "Whatever, Mom," he said turning around to watch television. He didn't want to hear what she had to say because he lost respect for her years ago and her opinion didn't mean shit to him. He was tired of hearing her nag like she really cared about him.

"Whatever my ass, and why ain't you in school?" she asked him. She knew if the caseworker found out he wasn't going to school, they might take her off welfare and she wasn't about to lose money over his bullshit.

"Nobody woke me up for school," he told her.

"You're grown now, so you can wake your own self up for school."

He was tired of going back and forth with her, so he just ignored her, knowing that this was the only way to get her to leave him alone.

"Ignore me if you want, but if you go to jail, I'm going to be the one doing the ignoring," she said going back upstairs to her room.

"Thank God," he said to himself when she was gone. He was tired of the way she always complained as if she really gave a fuck.

There was hardly ever any food in the fridge and the only reason he didn't starve to death growing up was the school lunches and the dinners that Grams used to cook for him before she moved.

He wondered what his brother and Grams were doing and he thought about calling them, but his mom had the number and he didn't feel like hearing her mouth.

The thought of food had his stomach growling and he realized that he hadn't eaten since breakfast. He got up and went to the fridge, hoping that there was something to eat, but all he saw was a box of baking soda and a pitcher of water. *Fuck*, he said to himself, slamming the door shut.

It was then that he remembered the money in his pocket and this made him smile. He walked into the living room and grabbed the AK from under the couch. After slinging it over his shoulder, he put on Blue's coat to make sure it didn't show.

When he looked in the mirror he nodded his head in approval. You could hardly tell that he was carrying the gun since Blue's coat was at least two sizes too big for him. After fixing the coat, he left the house and headed for Simi's to get something to eat.

He really missed Grams. She used to cook for him and Brandon every day around dinner time. Now it was just him and his moms, which equaled hard times. He thought about his family all the way to the store, wishing in his heart that he could have moved with them.

When he reached the restaurant, he ran into one of the OGs named Raw who always hung out on the corner.

"What's crackin', li'l CJ?" Raw asked as he walked up.

"I'm just trying to get something to snack on," CJ told him.

"I feel you, cuz. Just be careful out here."

"No doubt," CJ replied walking into the store. He knew how dangerous it was in his neighborhood, and if you weren't careful, catching a bullet while on your way to the store could become a reality.

He stood in line waiting his turn while some guy argued with the cashier.

"These wings ain't even done," the guy said.

"What you want me to do?" the cashier asked defensively.

"Give me my fucking money back."

"I can't do that, but I can get you a new batch of wings."

"I don't want no undone-ass wings, nigga. I want my dough."

"Well, I can't do that," the cashier told him arms raised in frustration.

"You know what," the man said picking up the food and throwing it at the cashier, "fuck this chicken and fuck that money. I got money, mothafucka." He pulled a hustler knot out of his pocket before storming out of the store.

When the man walked past, CJ saw an iced-out chain on his neck, an icy bracelet on one wrist and a nice iced-out watch on the other. Going straight into mode, he followed him out of the store to where his car was parked.

"Yo, cuz, you dropped something," he said causing the man to turn around.

When he was facing him, CJ lifted his AK from inside his coat and pointed it at the man.

"What the fuck is this?" the guy asked raising his hands.

"This is a robbery, nigga. Don't make it no murder," CJ answered cocking the AK back to let the man know there was one in the chamber.

"Nigga, do you know who the fuck I am? My name is Wicked, muthafucka. Larimer Avenue hoods nigga."

His words meant nothing to CJ and what he was saying would not save his life if he chose to not give up what CJ wanted.

"You going to be a dead man if you don't run them jewels and that bankroll in your pocket," CJ said letting the guy know that he didn't give a fuck who he was.

"You going to regret this," Wicked said taking his jewels off and emptying his pockets. When he was done, he handed everything over to CJ who was looking up and down the street for any signs of the police.

"Now get the fuck out of here," CJ said letting off a shot close to Wicked"s feet and causing him to jump in his car and pull off.

While he was robbing Wicked, Raw was across the street watching. When Wicked was gone, he crossed the street laughing. "Li'l cuz, you funny as hell," he said laughing at the way Wicked jumped in his car at the sound of the AK.

CJ didn't pay Raw any attention as he tucked the gun under his coat and began walking off to his house. He hoped that no one saw him pulling his little robbery, because he definitely wasn't trying to get knocked any time soon. He felt like he just found his purpose in life, which in his mind was sticking niggas up. The robbery thing seemed to come naturally to him and he knew that it would put him where he needed to be . . . at the top of the game.

He made it back to his house safe and sound and shook the thought of getting caught from his mind. After setting the AK on the living room couch, he took the money from his pocket and began to count it. He counted the money three times before putting it back in his pocket with the rest of his money. He couldn't believe that he made five stacks doing five minutes of work.

Next he took the jewels out of his pocket and put them on in front of the mirror. The chain kind of looked like the one his brother's dad left him, only his was white gold and it was a little icier. He knew that all of the jewels had to cost at least thirty thousand or more and, for a second, he thought about selling them. *Fuck that, I ain't selling shit*, he said to himself after admiring the jewels a little more. He looked like a rapper or something with all the bling on.

Before he could sit down, someone came knocking on the door. "Who is it?" he asked picking his gun up off the couch, just in case Wicked was coming back for retaliation.

"Open the door. It's Arab."

Arab was one of the few friends that he and Brandon had in the neighborhood. He was called Arab because he looked like he was from the Middle East—light skinned with curly hair, five foot two and about one hundred and twenty pounds. Even though he was a little guy, it didn't stop him from banging hard.

Arab was more into the streets than CJ was and was already crippin' like there was no tomorrow. His father and mother were alcoholics so he ran the streets day and night. On days when CJ was in the house preparing for school, he would sometimes see Arab though his window hustling on the corner.

"What's up with you, cuz?" he said letting Arab in the house.

"You what's up," Arab replied with a smile on his face.

"What you mean by that?"

"I heard you robbed Wicked and had him running out of the hood like a little bitch."

"Yeah, I got his bitch ass," CJ said nonchalantly like he had been robbing niggas on a regular basis.

"I wish I was there with you. I would have pistol whipped his bitch ass," Arab said pulling out his all black nine millimeter Ruger.

"You say it like you got a personal problem with the nigga."

"He a Larimer Avenue nigga and he shouldn't have been in our hood anyway. He think just 'cause he got a little money and put in work, he can go anywhere he please. For real, somebody should have been got him."

"Why didn't they?" CJ asked.

"Basically nobody wanted to start any beef, because it is hard to get money when you going to war. You just did what everybody else wanted to do."

"Well, fuck that nigga! He five stacks and some iced-out jewels lighter and if he want beef, then he can holler at me whenever."

"So you got him for five stacks?" Arab asked.

"Hell, yeah, and if I bump into him again, I'm going to take him for everything he own," CJ said ready to go all out. He was still feeling the adrenaline rush from the robbery and he was ready for more action.

"Next time you decide to rob somebody, let me know so I can come with you," Arab said just as Blue came walking into the house.

"What you doing in here, Arab?" Blue asked while moving the AK from the couch to the floor so he could sit down.

"I'm just kickin' it with CJ about the lick he hit."

"What lick?" Blue asked looking at CJ with a smile on his face.

"I robbed the nigga Wicked from Larimer for five stacks and these iced-out jewels," he said showing him the bling he had on.

"Damn, nigga, I leave for a split second and you already pulling robberies by yourself."

"The nigga was slipping, so I got him," he said as though it just had to happen.

Blue looked at him with a grin on his face and said, "I can't argue with that. If a nigga slip, then he got to get got."

Arab and CJ both nodded their heads in agreement, knowing what Blue said was true.

"So what you going to do with them jewels?" Blue asked wondering if he was going to sell them.

"I like the way they look on me, so I'm going to keep them."

"Just be careful because Wicked definitely going to try coming back about that shit," Blue said putting him up on game.

"I ain't worried about that bitch-ass nigga."

"Don't ever underestimate a nigga, no matter how much of a bitch he seem to be."

"Fuck that nigga," CJ said picking up the AK from the floor and setting it on his lap.

"So you loc'ed out now?" Blue asked smiling at him.

"It is what it is."

"Well, that's what we going to call you from now on...Li'l Loc."

He repeated the name to himself and decided that he liked the way it sounded.

"So you still up for tonight or you had enough for today?" Blue asked him.

"Can't never get enough."

"I see you already dressed for the occasion," Blue said pointing at Li'l Loc's attire.

"Yeah, I'm definitely ready." He had on all-black jeans and a black hoodie with some all-black Air Force Ones to match.

"So what you going to do?" Blue asked turning his attention to Arab.

"What you talking about?"

"You rolling with us tonight or what?" Blue asked already knowing that he was down for whatever they were about to get into.

"I'm definitely rolling."

"Do you need a strap or do you already got one?"

"I'm good," Arab said pulling his nine out.

"I should have known. Now I'm a-ask ya'll one more time, so ya'll don't feel like I'm forcing ya'll into this lifestyle. Are ya'll ready for this?"

Li'l Loc and Arab gave him a blank stare that let him know that they were more than ready.

"Let's ride out then," Blue said getting up from the couch and heading out the door with his goons following. They all got into Blue's Lexus and rode off into the night with money and a mission on their minds.

CHAPTER 11

As soon as school let out at two fifteen, they put the game on pause and began to discuss how they were going to set up shop after they got the work from CK Black. They both decided that once the rest of the homies got home, they would put them up on their plans and hope that they were all for it.

"You think them niggas get money saved up?" Pretty Boy asked Bay Boe.

"I know for sure them niggas be saving their money and I know them niggas is tired of being handed crumbs."

"If we play it smart, we will have the block on lock in no time," Pretty boy said thinking about what they were about to do.

"It's about that time, so let's go meet the homies at the bus stop. The faster we put everybody down, the faster we can get shit poppin'," Bay Boe said getting up to leave.

"I'm a-go check in with my grams first, then I'm going to meet you back here," Pretty Boy said following him out of the room.

As soon as they hit the corner, the bus pulled up and dropped everybody off. Bay Boe went to meet his homies as they got off the bus and Pretty Boy went to his house to check in with his grams.

"Grams," he hollered as he entered his house.

"Brandon, stop all that hollering. I'm in the kitchen."

He walked into the kitchen and was greeted by the smell of Grams' cooking.

"You hungry?" she asked him.

Although the smell of food had his stomach growling, he knew that he had to go handle some business. "I'm still full from them school lunches," he said lying through his teeth.

"I'll just put you up a plate for you to eat later."

"That's cool, because I'm headed to my friend's house around the corner," he told her ready to leave the house again.

"Make sure you be safe," was all she told him as he walked out the door.

He went straight to Bay Boe's house and knocked on the door.

"Who is it?" a female voice asked from the other side.

"It's Pretty Boy. Is Bay Boe there?" he asked.

The door opened up showing a frail woman who must have been Bay Boe's mother.

"He upstairs. Tell him I'm leaving out and make sure he locks the door when he leave," she said before shooting past him to go run the streets.

Pretty Boy walked in, locked the front door and headed upstairs to Bay Boe's room. He shouted Bay Boe's name as he neared the door, just to make sure he was in there.

"Come in, dog," Bay Boe replied.

Everybody greeted him as he walked in, showing him love as always.

"What up?" he replied dapping everybody up.

"I was just telling these niggas that it's our time to shine," Bay Boe told him as he sat on the couch.

"I feel you, but what you think the OGs going to say if we try to set up shop?" Snype asked knowing that they would have problems in that area.

"I ain't worried about them," Bay Boe said. He respected their OGs, but he was fed up with only getting crumbs for his hard work.

"They definitely going to be tripping about us stealing their dough flow," Mr. Boo said agreeing with Snype.

"No disrespect to them, but we be getting played anyway," Bay Boe told them.

"How you figure that?" Bundy asked not understanding where he was coming from.

"We're the ones making all the transactions and taking all the risk, so who you think going to jail? Us." He said answering his own question.

"So how are we going to do this?" LK asked feeling where Bay Boe was coming from.

"How much do ya'll niggas got saved up?" Bay Boe asked them.

"Two stacks," LK replied.

"Fifteen hundred," Bundy said.

"I got about five stacks," Boo said backing his homies.

"What about you, Snype?" Bay Boe asked hoping that he was down with the new move they were about to make.

"I got fifteen hundred," Snype answered confirming that he was down with whatever they were about to get into.

"Me and Pretty Boy got five thousand apiece, so that means we got twenty thousand all together. We can get a brick off of our connect for that much. On top of that we got six hand guns between us and we got the two AKs that Eight Ball was holding here."

"All we have to do now is round up the money so me and Bay Boe can go see the connect," Pretty Boy told them.

"Why only you and Pretty Boy get to go see the connect?" Bundy asked them not wanting to part with his money.

"You don't trust us?" Bay Boe asked him.

"Of course I trust ya'll," Bundy replied.

"Well, that's how the connect want it. If you got a problem with it, then keep making pennies on the block," Bay Boe told him.

"Fuck all that. Let's go grab this money so we can get this thing started," Mr. Boo said not caring who met the connect just as long as they got the work.

"Ya'll go handle that and come straight back," Bay Boe said dapping them up as they left.

As soon as the last of them was gone, Bay Boe opened his safe and took his money out. "Help me count this change," he said setting the money on the bed.

They counted the money twice just to make sure the count was right.

"We got eleven thousand here, which gives us a thousand to play with," Bay Boe said.

"I say let's go grab some walkie-talkies and a hooptie to get around in," Pretty Boy suggested.

"That sound like a good idea to me."

"Call CK Black and tell him we trying to see him," Pretty Boy said ready to get things moving.

"Bay Boe picked up the phone and dialed CK Black's number, and after the third ring he picked up.

"Who this?" CK Black asked not recognizing the number.

"It's Bay Boe and Pretty Boy. Remember we met you in Honus Wagner earlier today?"

"I remember ya'll niggas. What's poppin'?"

"We trying to come holler at you about what we discussed earlier."

"Do ya'll know how to get to Garfield?" CK asked.

"I know the way," Bay Boe told him.

"The address is 5236 Columbo Street. I'll see ya'll when ya'll get here."

"We on our way."

"One," CK replied breaking the connection.

"What he say?" Pretty Boy asked anxious to know if the deal was one.

"He want us to meet him on Columbo."

"You think we going to have some problems?"

"We should be good because they Blood over there. But just in case, we going to take these two thirty-shot Glocks for 'em," he said patting the strap on his waist.

Remembering the gun he had made Pretty Boy feel much better about the move they were making.

Ten minutes later everybody was back at the house with their money. Bay Boe set the money on his bed and began to count it. The last thing he wanted to do was short CK Black by accident on their first transaction.

"It's twenty thousand on the nose," he said putting the money in a Honus Wagner bag. After making sure everything was straight, he called a jitney to take them to Garfield.

While they were waiting for the jitney, the whole room was silent, each of them wrapped up in their own thoughts. All of them were contemplating the good and bad about what they were about to get into. If everything went right, then they would be on top. But if shit went bad, they would all be back at square one starting from the bottom, and it would be a hard grind now that Eight was gone, so their new move had to work.

It didn't take long for the jitney to come, and as soon as they heard the car out front beeping the horn, they got up to leave.

"Ya'll niggas sit tight until we get back," Bay Boe said picking his gun up from the bed and putting it in his waist band.

"Be careful," LK said hooking the PlayStation up and the rest of the homies said the same.

Pretty Boy and Bay Boe went outside and got into the waiting car. "So where we headed to, boss?" the jitney driver asked them.

"5326 Columbo Street out Garfield," Bay Boe told him.

"That's going to be seven dollars up front and fourteen if ya'll want me to bring ya'll back."

Bay Boe gave him the fourteen up front and told him he would give him extra to wait for them.

"That's cool with me," the jitney driver replied pulling off.

About ten minutes later they pulled up in the Columbo projects and Pretty Boy tensed up at the sight of all the Bloods standing outside. The fact that they were carrying twenty thousand dollars in cash didn't help either.

"You sure this is cool?" he asked nervously.

"Of course it's cool. These niggas is Bloods and even if they do trip, somebody going to die when this Glock go off."

"This is the address right here," the driver said pulling over. "Ya'll not going to be long are ya'll?" he asked feeling just as uncomfortable as they were.

"Nah . . . but if we do take long, I will pay you extra," Bay Boe told him before hopping out of the car with the bag full of money in one hand and his other hand on the handle of his Glock.

Pretty Boy got out on the other side and stood on the sidewalk with his hand on his gun as well, looking for any signs of trouble. When Bay Boe came around to his side, they walked together towards the address CK Black gave them.

As they walked through the large crowd in front of CK Black's spot, one of the Bloods stood in front of them blocking their path.

They thought they were going to have to start shooting, and they both tightened their grips on the handles of the guns under their shirts.

"What set ya'll claim?" the Blood asked grilling them.

"The Hill District, 1800 block Bedford Avenue Bloods, five all the time," Bay Boe replied throwing his set up.

After seeing that they were Blood, the crowd parted to let them through. They continued on through the crowd until they reached CK's front door.

After knocking, a female answered from the inside. "Who is it?" she asked before opening up.

"It's Bay Boe and Pretty Boy. We here to see CK Black," Bay Boe said.

Two minutes later, just when they were about to turn around and leave, the door opened up.

"What up, Blood?" CK said letting them in.

"What up?" they both replied walking into the house. They stood close to the door and scanned their surroundings, still being cautious.

"Make yourselves comfortable," he said pointing to the couch. He saw that they were a little uptight and he was trying to let them know that everything was gravy. "Ya'll ain't have no problems out there?"

"We was cool," Bay Boe replied not wanting him to know how nervous they really were.

"Good, because I told them some young Hill niggas was coming to see me. As soon as the words were out of his mouth, someone hit him on his walkie-talkie.

"You good in there?" the voice asked.

"Yeah, I'm good. These is my young Hill niggas," he replied back into the walkie-talkie. "I got these projects on lock, and nobody can get in or out without my approval," he told them.

They both nodded their heads, amazed at how organized CK Black ran his business and his hood.

"So what can I do for ya'll?" CK asked them ready to get down to business.

"We trying to grab a whole bird," Pretty Boy said with a serious look on his face that let CK Black know he was about his business.

"Ya'll know I need twenty thousand for that."

"We got it," Bay Boe said tapping the Honus Wagner bag.

CK Black was surprised. They were so young, he thought they were going to come wanting only an ounce. "Come with me," he said walking into the dining room.

Bay Boe followed behind him and Pretty Boy, staying back a little with his hand on his Glock just in case it was a set up.

When they reached the dining room, they sat at the table while CK Black went into the drop ceiling and pulled out the work.

As they watched, he took out a block of powder cocaine and set it down on the table in front of them. "That's a key right there. Do ya'll know how much it is suppose to weigh?" he asked them.

"A thousand grams," Bay Boe answered.

"A thousand is right," CK said pulling out his triple beam scale. He weighed the coke up in front of them to let them know it was official.

They both looked at the scale and nodded their heads in approval.

"Now, do ya'll know how to cook this shit up?" he asked.

They both shook their heads no.

"I'm a-give ya'll a quick lesson in whipping up and getting extras, so pay close attention. If ya'll do it like I show ya'll, then ya'll should get at least an extra two hundred grams off of ya'll key, but this depends on how good ya'll want it to be. Ya'll following me?" he asked, making sure he still had their attention.

"We following you," Pretty Boy said letting him know that they were catching on.

"Watch closely," he told them while pulling out an ounce of powder coke, some baking soda, a Pyrex jar, a pot and a tray of ice cubes.

He put the half ounce of baking soda into the jar with an ounce of cocaine and mixed it up real good, adding only a little bit of water. After putting the water in the pot, he put the Pyrex in the middle and sat the pot on top of the stove.

Next he turned the flame up and watched the water boil as he stirred the coke into the baking soda, whipping it like it was cake batter. After about ten minutes of whipping, the mixture turned oily.

He then took the Pyrex out of the pot and ran some cool water over the mixture, making it turn hard. He also put a few ice cubes into the jar to help the hardening process.

When he saw that it was done, he dropped the crack on a plate in front of them. "What ya'll think?" he asked.

"Piece of cake," Pretty Boy replied. He had caught on to everything CK showed him. Bay Boe, on the other hand, was clueless and he figured that he would leave the cooking up to his homie.

Ya'll good to go then," he said tossing the bird of coke into Bay Boe's lap before going back into the ceiling to grab another. He handed this one to Pretty Boy and let them know that they owed him twenty thousand dollars for the additional key.

"When do you want to be paid for it?" Pretty Boy asked looking down at the coke in his lap.

"I ain't in no rush, so when ya'll get it, then get at me."

"Don't you want to count the money?" Bay Boe asked him.

"Just dump it on the table and put them keys in the bag. I'll see ya'll next time ya'll score," he said letting them know that they had his trust.

They threw the work in the Honus Wagner bag and got up to leave. As they were walking past him to exit the kitchen, he noticed the chain on Pretty Boy's neck and it reminded him of someone he knew, so he questioned him about it.

"Yo, Pretty Boy . . . where did you get that chain from?" he asked trying to remember exactly who he had seen wearing it before.

"My dad left it to me when he passed away."

CK was about to ask him who his dad was when the female who let them in interrupted their conversation.

"There's somebody else out here who need to see you," she told him.

"I'm coming right now," CK said dropping the subject to lead them to the front door. "Get at me when ya'll ready," he told them as they left.

"For sure," Bay Boe said heading back to the waiting jitney.

They were just as paranoid as they had been when they walked in. Even though they knew nobody would try them, they were still leery of the crowd in front of CK Black's spot. When they got in the car, they felt a little better even though they had a long way to go before they were home free.

"Ya'll good to go?" the jitney driver asked making sure they were done with their business before pulling off.

"Yeah, we good," Bay Boe said handing him an extra fifty bucks for the wait.

The whole ride back to Bay Boe's house had them sweating bullets. They knew that if they got pulled over with what they were carrying, it would be a one-way ticket to juvenile life for both of them.

When they got to Bay Boe's spot, it was a relief. Before they got out of the car, the jitney driver gave them a card and told them to call his cell phone if they needed to make another trip.

Bay Boe took the card and went into his house with Pretty Boy following behind, searching up and down the street for any signs of the police. As soon as they entered the house, they were hit with a barrage of questions.

"Did ya'll get it?" LK asked concerned about their money.

"Please tell me ya'll didn't get robbed," Bundy said already thinking the worst.

"Where the work at?" Boo asked hoping that everything went the way it was supposed to.

Bay Boe smiled at them and dumped the two keys of coke on the floor for them to see.

"What the fuck is this?" LK asked picking one up. He had never seen raw cocaine before and to him it looked like some blow up because it was hard and soda like.

"That's cocaine, nigga!" Pretty Boy said excited about the move they were about to make. He knew that they were about to go straight to the top and he couldn't wait to get started.

"What we supposed to do with it?" Bundy asked examining the other bird.

"The connect showed us how to cook it up, and if we do it right, we will get extra grams," Bay Boe told them.

Since none of them had seen raw cocaine before, they each passed the coke around to inspect it.

"Let's get this shit cooked up," Mr. Boo said after every-body examined the work.

"I got this," Pretty Boy said grabbing the two birds. "Is it cool to use your kitchen?" he asked Bay Boe.

"My mom don't give a fuck, but we going to have to give her some hard to leave us alone."

"Aiight," Pretty Boy said.

They all went downstairs to the kitchen to get things together so they could begin to cook the coke up.

"Do you got a Pyrex jar?" Pretty Boy asked.

"It's in the cupboard," Bay Boe said grabbing it for him. He also went around grabbing everything else they would need, including a digital scale.

"Where you get all this stuff from?" Snype asked wondering why he had all the stuff needed to cook coke on hand.

"Eight Ball use to whip up coke here, and he had me holding a bunch of stuff for him in case he needed it."

Pretty Boy took the scale and weighed up one hundred twenty-five grams of cocaine and busted it down to turn it into powder. Then he took the coke and mixed it with sixty-five grams of baking soda and put it in the Pyrex, adding just the right amount of water to the mixture.

After that he took the Pyrex and set it in the middle of a pot filled halfway with water. He turned on the flame and when the water started to boil in the pot and the Pyrex, he began to stir the mixture like he was a professional.

"You sure that you know what you doing?" Bundy asked looking at the oily substance in the pot.

"I got this," Pretty Boy replied. When he saw the coke forming, he got some cool water on it and hit it with two ice cubes. The water and the ice turned it solid, and it came out looking just like the mixture CK Black cooked up.

They let the work dry out on a paper towel then put it on the scale. The crack weighed one hundred, fifty grams, which meant they had an extra twenty-five grams.

"Damn, nigga, you a magician," Bay Boe said looking at the scale.

"Just call me Chef Boyardee," Pretty Boy said smiling.

"You definitely the chef, so finish cheffin' the rest of this so we can put it on the market," Bay Boe told him.

He went back to whipping the coke up while everybody watched with anticipation, thinking in their heads about what they had to do once the coke was ready.

CHAPTER 12

I t took two hours to whip the coke up and Pretty Boy was
happy to be done. He was sweating from slaving over the
stove, but he knew that the worst was yet to come. They got an
extra seven ounces and a quarter, which gave them forty-three
ounces and a quarter of hard.

Now everybody was at the dining room table bagging the work
up. They were only bagging up twenty dollar pieces that weighed a
half of a gram each, which was much bigger than everybody else's
on their block, so they knew that they were going to lock shit
down.

In the middle of bagging up, Bay Boe's mom walked in the
room and saw what they were doing. She immediately started
tripping, going off on everybody in the room.

"What ya'll doing in my house with all of this shit?" she asked
with an attitude.

"Come on with that bullshit, Mom. You see we doing business
in here!" Bay Boe replied not trying to hear her mouth.

"Ya'll got to break me off something for using my house," she
said staring at all the crack on the table.

Bay Boe didn't want to keep arguing with her, so he grabbed
the extra quarter off the table and gave her a half gram. He also let
her know that they would be selling them for twenty dollars if
anybody wanted to cop something.

"Twenty dollars for all this?"

"You heard me right."

It must be some bullshit, she said to herself while going up the
steps to her room.

"Your moms be tripping," LK said when she was gone.

"Hopefully that piece I gave her will keep her out of our way,"
Bay Boe said shaking his head at his mom's actions. There was a
time in his life when he was ashamed of his mom's habit, but after

being in the streets for a while, he stopped giving a fuck. He just vowed to himself that he would never become strung out like her.

After about five minutes, his mom came back down the steps.

"What you want now?" Bay Boe asked, hoping that she wasn't on any bullshit.

"Who you get this shit off?" she asked him with her eyes beaming.

"What's wrong with it?" he asked her thinking that she was running some of her game.

"Ain't nothing wrong with it. This is the best shit out here. Give me another piece so I can let Knobby try it out."

"What you think I'm a fool or something?" Bay Boe asked giving her a come-on look.

"Boy, I'm being serious. You know that Knobby got a lot of clientele and if she like it, she will spend a lot of money with ya'll."

"Aiight, Mom," he said giving her another twenty piece. She left the house telling them she would be back, but Bay Boe didn't plan on it.

"Ma Dukes is brazzy," LK said laughing.

Even though Bay Boe's mom got high, everybody still respected her. Also, she gave them a lot of game whenever she wasn't running around chasing drugs.

"Forget about her. Let's just finish bagging this shit up. If it's as good as she say it is, then we going to kill the block," Bay Boe told them.

As soon as they finished bagging up, Bay Boe's mom came back in the house with her friend Knobby following close behind.

"I told ya'll I'd be back," she said walking into the dining room.

"So who got that good crack in here?" Knobby asked holding a hundred dollar bill in her hand.

"Give her six of them dubs," Bay Boe told Snype.

"We selling them for twenty dollars apiece, but since you spending a hundred, I'm giving you six," Snype told her.

"If ya'll selling these at twenty dollars apiece, I'm a-bring ya'll some business. Just make sure ya'll look out for me when I come back," she said looking at the jumbo twenties in her hand.

"We definitely got you," Bay Boe told her.

"Just be on standby," she said leaving the house with Bay Boe's mom.

Another two hours passed and they were done bagging up all of the work.

"We got twenty-four hundred dubs," Pretty Boy said after counting them. "That's forty-eight thousand if we take straight money, but just to make them go fast we going to do two for thirty-fives or three for fifties. Hopefully we should come out with around forty-two thousand."

"So how we going to set this shit up?" Mr. Boo asked.

"I've been thinking and I feel like we would be better off hustling from here instead of standing on Front Street. Just to be safe, we could keep the dubs in bundles of one hundred and only keep one bundle in the house at a time," Bay Boe suggested.

"What about the walkie-talkies we was talking about earlier?" Pretty Boy reminded him.

"I'm a-run downtown and grab some walkie-talkies, a scanner and two surveillance monitors. Bundy and LK…ya'll can monitor whoever comes on the street and whoever leaves out," Bay Boe told them.

"Boo, you on stash patrol, which means whenever the stash get low, you have to run back out and grab more work. Pretty Boy, you going to be watching the surveillance monitors and listening to the scanner. If you hear about any bust in the area, we going to shut down shop and bring Bundy and LK back in the house till shit calm all the way down," Bay Boe said informing them of their positions.

"What about me?" Snype asked feeling left out.

"You the money man. After every bundle gets sold, take the money to your house and put it in the safe until we get ready to re-up. That way if our spot get hit, they won't find too much drugs or large sums of money."

"So how are we going to split the profits up?" Bundy asked.

"We going to split the profits evenly off of the one bird, but the profits from the other key goes back into the flip. So do anybody got any objections about what I put together?" he asked looking around the room.

"It sound good to me," Snype said and everybody else nodded in agreement.

"Well, let's put this shit in motion," he said standing up. "I'm going to call a jitney and go get all the surveillance shit we need. Meanwhile ya'll niggas put these dubs in bundles of a hundred and sit tight till I get back."

It didn't take long for the jitney to come. After he left, Ma Dukes, which is what everybody called Bay Boe's mom, came walking in the door with Knobby and a few customers.

"Who got them boulders?" one of the customers—commonly known as "snaps"—asked.

"It's right here," Pretty Boy said waving them over to the table.

All of the snaps got six for a hundred, totaling three hundred. After copping, they all left promising to be back.

A half hour went past and they made one thousand, seven hundred and fifty from one of the bundles of dubs. Snype was leaving the house to go put up the money and almost ran into Bay Boe on his way out the door.

"Where he going?" Bay Boe asked Pretty Boy who was serving a snap in the dining room.

"We sold one of them bundles, so he is going to put the money up," Pretty Boy answered.

"The spot jumpin' like that?" Bay Boe asked surprised.

"Hell, yeah," Pretty Boy said pocketing the money he just made from the sell before walking the snaps he served to the front door.

"If everything go right, we will move these two birds in no time," Bay Boe said passing out the walkie-talkies to everyone. He also gave Pretty Boy a scanner and showed him how to work it. After seeing that he would be cool, he went upstairs to his room and grabbed the two hundred-round AKs out of his closet for LK and Bundy. He made sure they were loaded and went back downstairs.

"Damn, dog, where the fuck Eight Ball get these from?" Bundy asked examining the rifle in his had.

"Don't even worry about that. Just make sure you on point out there," Bay Boe told him.

"Where we suppose to post up at?" LK asked.

"Both of ya'll find a cut on each corner at the end of this street. If someone comes on the street looking shady, leave 'em holy like the bible," Bay Boe told them.

"We got you," LK replied leaving the house to go play the corner with Bundy.

As soon as they got situated, they radioed back in to let everybody know that they were on point.

"Aiight, dog, ya'll just be safe and if ya'll see Handy Man Jack, send him to the spot, so he can put these cameras up for us."

"No doubt," they both answered.

Handy Man was a known crack head who could fix anything, and would fix it for a little bit of crack. About ten minutes later, Handy Man came past the house and put the cameras up for them. Now they were officially up and running.

They let Handy Man know that they would get at him if they needed him. As Handy Man was on his way out the door, Snype was coming back in.

"What took you so long?" Pretty Boy asked him.

"My raise was cooking, so I sat down and had a bite."

"Just remember, nigga, business first," Pretty Boy said, handing him another one thousand, seven hundred and fifty dollars wrapped up in a rubber band.

"Ya'll knocked another bundle that quick?"

"Yeah, nigga. That's why we need you to be on point at all times."

"I feel you," Snype said taking the money and heading back out the door.

Things went on like this all day. Bundy and LK radioed in telling them when the cops were out so they could shut down shop till the block cooled down. But when everything cleared up, they were right back at it.

They hustled all through the weekend, telling their parents that they were spending the night at Bay Boe's house playing video games. In reality they were pulling all nighters getting money. By Monday morning they had cooked up and sold the last of their coke, making eighty-four thousand dollars. They took the sixty thousand and put it to the side for when they re-up and they split the other twenty thousand evenly, which was four thousand apiece.

"I can't believe we made all this money so fast," LK said counting his profits.

"Just think, we got the cheapest coke on the Hill and it's the best. On top of that, our shop stay open all night. While niggas be at the club or with their hoes, we grinding," Bay Boe said making all the sense in the world.

"Now we got to prepare for the haters," Pretty Boy told them, knowing that the problems were soon to come.

"I forgot to tell ya'll that the nigga Phabobe stopped me when I was making a money run and asked if he could holler at our connect," Snype told them.

"What you say?" Bay Boe asked.

"I told him that I never met the connect, and then he asked me if I could get him a quarter bird of soft."

"I wouldn't mind selling him a eighty, but not right now. I feel that we should take advantage of this block money and once we get our change right, then we can sell weight," Bay Boe told them.

"We should at least give it a month before we start serving hustlers. By then our spot will be hot anyway and only selling weight will take the heat off of us," LK said agreeing with Bay Boe.

"Just to keep niggas from hating, let's shut down shop at two in the morning on school nights and open up when school let out, but when the weekend come, we go hard," Pretty Boy suggested.

Everybody agreed with each other on how to run the spot, and all the homies except for Pretty Boy and Bay Boe had school the next day so they got ready to leave.

"I'm out," LK said standing up. He knew that if he stayed any longer, he would not be going to school the next day.

"Me, too," Bundy said yawning.

Snype and Mr. Boo got up as well.

"As soon as the sun rise, me and Pretty Boy going to meet the connect, so when school let out, we will have more work," Bay Boe said walking his homies to the door.

"See ya'll niggas tomorrow," Pretty Boy said dapping everybody up before they left.

After they left, Pretty Boy got ready to leave as well since he had to check in on his grams. Anyway, he was still acting like he had to go to school in the morning.

"In the A.M.," Bay Boe said dapping him up.

"In the A.M.'" Pretty Boy replied as he left.

When he got to his house, he went straight to his grams' room to see if she was still up. "Grams, you up?" he whispered into her room.

"Yes, I'm awake."

He knew that she must have been real worried about him because usually she didn't wait up when he stayed out late.

"I'm just letting you know that I'm home," he said easing her worried mind.

"Do you want me to wake you in the morning?" she asked.

"Definitely," he replied knowing that he wouldn't be able to get up on his own.

"Well, I'll see you in the morning."

"Aiight, Grams, good night," he said before going to his room.

Once in his room, he took out his clothes for the next day, which consisted of an all-black Dickie suit, black Air Force Ones and an all-black Pirate's fitted cap. When he was done laying out his outfit, he pulled the money he made over the weekend from his pocket and began to count it.

After counting out the four stacks, he put a rubber band around it and put it inside an empty shoe box. He then slid the shoe box under his bed and laid down. Seconds later he drifted off to sleep with money on his mind.

*   *   *   *

The next morning Grams woke him up and, strangely, he didn't have another bad dream. He got up, took a shower and got dressed. After looking in the mirror as he always did to check his swag, he nodded his head in satisfaction. Next he went to Grams' room to let her know that he was leaving.

"Be good, baby," she told him before he left her room.

He then left the house and headed to the bus stop. When he got there, he greeted all of his homies.

"You ready to go grab this work?" Baby Boe asked him.

"I'm more than ready," he replied.

"Damn, Pretty Boy, you can't speak?" Ki-Ki asked interrupting their conversation.

He turned from Bay Boe and faced her. "What up, sexy?" he asked her with a smile on his face.

"I thought we was going to talk on Friday, but you stood me up," she said smiling.

"My fault. It's just I was busy all weekend," he told her not going into the specifics of what he was doing.

"Well, when you going to have some time for me?"

"The bus won't be here for another five to ten minutes, so we can talk a little now," he told her.

"Well, when you going to be my boyfriend?" she asked catching him off guard.

"I thought you didn't mess with niggas who gangbang?"

"I don't, but I'll make an exception for you."

"Why the change of heart?"

"Well, I really like you and I think you are a good person. Any way, I don't think that you would ever do me wrong."

He was satisfied with her answer and he was glad that she finally came around to like him. "Of course I'll be your man, and I promise I'll take care of you," he said staring into her pretty hazel eyes.

She could tell that he meant every word he said by the way he looked at her.

"The bus is coming, Ki-Ki," one of her friends said interrupting their little moment.

"When you get off school, come pass Bay Boe's house so we can talk a little more."

"Aiight," she said smiling at her man as she got on the bus.

"Come on, Ike, we got business to handle," Bay Boe said as the bus pulled away from the curb.

"Let's go," Pretty Boy said following him to his house.

When they got there, it was straight to business. Bay Boe opened the safe and pulled the re-up money out.

"Let's count this money to make sure it's straight," he said setting the dough on his bed.

"This is a lot of change," Pretty Boy said eyeing all the cash they had.

"Just think how much more we going to make," Bay Boe replied taking a large stack to count.

Pretty Boy grabbed a couple stacks of money and began to count as well.

It took them about thirty minutes to make sure the money was right.

"How much you got over there?" Bay Boe asked.

"Thirty-three thousand on the nose,"

"I got twenty-seven thousand, which means the money is straight. Let's chill for another two hours and then call CK Black to let him know that we ready to score."

"Well, while we waiting set the game up so I can trash you," Pretty Boy said wanting to avenge the ass beating he got the last time they played.

"Nigga, you couldn't beat me blindfolded," Bay Boe replied laughing.

They played *Madden* for two hours going back and forth talking shit. After losing his second game in a row, Bay Boe put the controller down. "Nigga, you got me. But enough of these games, we got business to handle."

"What time is it?" Pretty Boy asked.

Bay Boe looked down at his watch and was surprised at how long they had been bullshitting around. "It's a little after ten o'clock."

Pretty Boy took the phone off the hook and handed it to him, so he could make the call.

"Who this?" CK answered after the second ring.

"It's your little homies from the Hill," Bay Boe told him.

"What's good with ya'll?"

"We done with that and we trying to come holler at you."

"Ya'll done already?" CK asked surprised.

"Yeah, we ran through that shit,"

"Ya'll can come through right now then."

"We on our way," Bay Boe told him before hanging up.

"What he say?" Pretty Boy asked.

"He want us to come through," Bay Boe said while trying to call a jitney.

Pretty Boy began putting the money in a Honus Wagner bag as Bay Boe listed to the phone ringing.

After the tenth ring, he hung up the phone.

"What's wrong?" Pretty Boy asked seeing the frustrated look on his face.

"I can't get a fucking jitney."

"What about the one we called last time?" Pretty Boy said grabbing his card from the top of the television.

"I forgot about him," Bay Boe said taking the card and dialing the number. He got an answer after the third ring.

"Jitney service. Mr. Ray speaking."

"Mr. Ray . . . it's the two guys that you took to Garfield."

"I'm on my way," he told Bay Boe knowing that their money was good.

Bay Boe hung the phone up and turned to Pretty Boy. "He on his way, so we might as well go downstairs and wait."

Even though they knew that CK Black was cool, they still took their guns just to be on the safe side. They both knew that when you are in the game, it's better to be safe than sorry.

It didn't take long for Mr. Ray to show up and when he did, they left the house to handle their business.

"What up, Mr. Ray?" they both said as they got in the car.

"What up, young bucks? Where we headed to this time?" he asked them.

"Same place as last time," Bay Boe told him.

"Garfield it is then," he said pulling off.

After twenty minutes of driving, they pulled up in the Columbo projects and they were even more nervous than the last time they scored. The projects were packed. There were twice as many people out and this made them feel real uncomfortable.

They hopped out in front of the spot, both of them holding on to the butt of their guns. But this time, the crowd parted without any problems.

"What up, Blood?" a few of them said remembering them from the last time they came through.

"What up, Ike?" they both replied as they walked to CK Black's front door. Before they could knock, the door opened and CK Black was there to user them into the house.

"What up, li'l homies?" he asked them as they stood in the living room.

"How you know that we was out front?" Bay Boe asked.

CK Black pointed at his new surveillance monitors. "I just got them off of one of my young niggas yesterday. I don't really need them because my goons stay on point with the walkie-talkies, but they was cheap."

"We got some in our spot, too," Bay Boe said checking them out.

"So what can I do for ya'll?" CK Black asked leading them into the dining room.

"We got the twenty stacks we owe you and another forty to spend," Pretty Boy told him.

He went into the drop ceiling, pulled out four birds and put them on the table for them to see. "Ya'll can handle this, right?"

"We got it," Bay Boe said putting the coke inside the Honus Wagner bag after dumping the money on the table.

"I got a couple moves to make, so I'm a-catch up with ya'll later. If ya'll need anything like guns or bullet-proof vest, let me know," he said walking them to the door.

"We probably grab some vest off you the next time we come through," Pretty Boy told him.

"Just let me know," he said as they left.

They walked back to the car with their hands on their guns still leery of the crowd. When they got back in the jitney, Pretty Boy gave Mr. Ray one hundred dollars for the wait and told him to drive cautiously, meaning not too fast and not too slow. Mr. Ray strapped on his seat belt and drove the speed limit all the way to the Hill District.

It was a long ride to Bay Boe's house, and what made it feel even longer was the four bricks in their possession. Every time they passed a cop car, both of them prayed silently that they didn't get pulled over. When they got to the house, Bay Boe hopped out of the ride and went straight in with the work.

Pretty Boy let Mr. Ray know that they would call him the next time they needed him. He then got out of the car and went into the house as well.

Bay Boe was in the kitchen waiting for him. "Let's get this shit cooked up," he said as soon as Pretty Boy walked in the room.

Pretty Boy was on it. He went around the kitchen gathering all the things he would need to whip the coke. After he got everything prepared, he began performing the task at hand.

"How long you think it's going to take to cook all this shit up?" Bay Boe asked him.

"It's going to be a while," Pretty Boy replied, mixing nine ounces of cocaine with four and a half ounces of baking soda.

"I'm a-go grab some bomb then . . . you want anything?"

"Grab me a Pepsi and a few bags of chips."

"I got you, dog," Bay Boe said leaving the house. He went to one of his homie's spots and grabbed a quarter of haze and an ounce of fifty (mid-grade) for two hundred twenty-five dollars. After that he stopped at the store and grabbed a few blunts, some pops and a couple bags of chips. He knew that they would not have time to go get something to eat with all the coke they had to cook up.

The pops and chips were like a hustler's meal—good for when you are on the go and great for the stomach. When he got back to the house, Pretty Boy was just getting started with the process of cooking up, and he knew that it would be a while before he was finished. He didn't want to be in the way, so he sat in the living room and began rolling up. Anyway, the rancid smell of cooking up wasn't something that he could get used to.

So for the next few hours, he smoked and watched the surveillance monitors, only bothering his homie when it was time to pass the weed.

CHAPTER 13

Driving through the streets in Blue's Lexus made them feel like they were on top of the world. Everybody they passed in the streets stopped and stared. Some were in awe and some were in fear, praying that the notorious Blue didn't pull over and terrorize their block. What made it even worse was he had two young niggas in the car with him who looked even hungrier than he did.

Blue drove all the way to the West Side of Pittsburgh and pulled over in the Greenway projects. "This is it," he said getting out of the car.

Arab and Li'l Loc got out as well and they all huddled up on the driver's side of the car.

"What's the plan?" Arab asked anxious to put in some work.

"I'm a-knock on the door and go in like I'm trying to buy some weed. Once I'm inside, ya'll kick in the door with mask and gloves on and lay me and her down. After ya'll do that, she going to let ya'll know where the stash is at. When ya'll get it, run back to the car and I'll be right behind ya'll."

"How you know she holding work in there?" Li'l Loc asked hoping that he wasn't on a ghost mission.

"I use to fuck with the bitch's best friend and the last time I was over there I seen the bitch putting the pounds up."

"How many pounds you think she got in there?" Arab asked.

"Don't worry about it. Just do it right and remember the bitch know me, so make it seem as if I don't got nothing to do with this shit."

"We got you," Li'l Loc assured him.

After seeing that he got his point across and that they understood the plan, he went up to the house and knocked on the door. A few seconds passed before a female opened the door and let him in.

"What up with you, Tiff?" he asked walking into her house.

"I'm just up here trying to move this weed. What's up with you? If you looking for Keisha, I have not seen her today."

"I ain't looking for Keish. I'm just trying to grab some of that tree," he said, pulling a couple hundred out of his pocket.

"Don't nobody got weed on your side of town?" she asked wondering why he traveled all the way across town just to buy some weed.

"It's dry as hell in Homewood and the niggas who do got it is selling some bullshit," he told her.

"Well, how much is you trying to buy?"

Before he could get it out, Arab and Li'l Loc came crashing through the door. They put their guns to both Tiff and Blue, laying them down on the ground.

"Where the shit at, bitch?" Arab screamed smacking her in the face with his gun.

"I don't know what you talking about."

This brought another blow to the face, busting her lip wide open.

"Just tell them where the shit is before they kill us!" Blue screamed as if in fear for his life.

"Okay, okay…it's upstairs in my bedroom. Just please don't kill me," she screamed while crying hysterically.

"Where in the bedroom?" Li'l Loc asked.

"It's in back of the closet," she told them.

Arab ran upstairs to the bedroom and went into the closet. It didn't take him more than thirty seconds to find the two duffle bags reeking of weed. "Jackpot," he said opening the bags to reveal at least a hundred pounds of mid-grade weed. He closed the bag and ran back downstairs to let Li'l Loc know that he found the stash.

"We out," Li'l Loc said signaling for him to come on.

"Nah, fuck that," Arab said smacking Tiff in the face once again with his nine. This time he broke her nose and the pain she was feeing was excruciating. "Bitch, where the money at?" he asked her.

"What money?" she answered trying to play dumb.

"I'm a-just kill her," Li'l Loc said putting the AK to her head and cocking it back.

"Please tell them where the money at before he kill you," Blue said as if he was concerned for her safety.

Tiff knew that she was already going to be in some shit for losing the weed and she didn't want to give them the money. So when Blue made this comment, she just stared at him with hate in her eyes wishing he would shut the fuck up.

Li'l Loc was tired of playing games with her, so he let off a shot right next to her head.

She let out a loud scream and began to cry even harder. "The money is in the kitchen cabinet behind the box of oatmeal. It's wrapped up in Saran," she said praying that they let her live. "It's at least twenty grand, but I swear it's all I have."

Arab ran into the kitchen and grabbed the money out of the cabinet. "Now let's be out," he said entering the living room with the money in hand.

"Thank God," Tiff said happy that they were finally leaving.

"Bitch, shut the fuck up and listen good. If you call the police, I swear I will come back and blow your brains out," Li'l Loc said pointing the AK at her.

"I understand," she relplied with fear in her voice.

"And you empty your pockets, nigga," Arab said pointing his gun at Blue.

"Come on, man, this is all the money I got," Blue said playing his part.

"I don't give a fuck, nigga. Either give the money or get a bullet," Arab told him.

"Aiight, cuz," Blue said pulling the knot out of this pocket.

After getting the money from Blue, Arab and Li'l Loc ran out of the house.

As soon as they were gone, Blue got up off the floor. "Bitch, you almost got us killed with your bullshit," he said while brushing his clothes off.

"Nigga, it ain't my fault I got robbed," she said picking up the phone to call her boy friend who was responsible for all the pounds in her house.

Blue saw her dialing a number and he flipped. "What the fuck is you doing?" he asked hoping that she wasn't calling the police.

"I'm calling my muthafucking boy friend," she replied, fed up with Blue.

"I'm out of here then," he said leaving her in the house to face her problems on her own.

He ran down the hill with a smile on his face. When he got to his car, he found Arab and Li'l Loc ducked down in the backseat.

"Ya'll good?" he asked while starting the car up.

"Yeah, we good," Li'l Loc replied as they pulled off.

"We going to count everything up when we get back to the hood," Blue told them.

On their way back o Homewood, the words of Li'l Turk rang in their ears, that head bussa music.

The three of them knew that they would live and die by the words coming out of the stereo. When they got back to Li'l Loc's house, they began splitting up the weed and money.

"One hundred pounds and twenty thousand dollars!" Blue said smiling at the success of their robbery.

Li'l Loc and Arab couldn't believe it. They were only sixteen and they had more money than most people twice their age.

"That's six thousand and thirty-three pounds apiece. Anything extra I keep, being as though it was my lick," Blue said pausing in case there were any objections.

"Cool with me, cuz," Li'l Loc said pocketing his easily earned money.

Arab felt the same way and he didn't object either.

"So when we going to hit another lick?" Li'l Loc asked ready to put more money in his pocket.

"You have to get rid of what you get first," Blue told him.

"Who I'm a-sell it to?"

"I know a few people who might want to buy some pounds. I'll holler at them first thing tomorrow."

"Sound good to me," Arab replied not wanting to have to hit the block to sell his weed.

"What about you, Li'l Loc?"

"Yeah, that sound good," Li'l Loc answered. He didn't care how the weed got sold as long as it got sold.

"I'm a-get at ya'll in the A.M.," Blue said putting his pounds in a garbage bag and going upstairs to Li'l Loc's mom's room.

Arab pulled a box of dutchees out of his pocket and began cracking one, preparing to roll up some of the good weed they had.

Li'l Loc watched silently, wondering in his head what the big deal was about smoking weed. On the commercial they always said that it killed brain cells, but Arab and Blue seemed pretty cool to him.

When Arab was done rolling up, he looked at Li'l Loc. "You want to hit this?" he asked him.

"You know I don't smoke."

"I know, but this is a celebration so it's only right."

Li'l Loc thought about it and decided that one time wouldn't hurt. He didn't know that weed was a highly addictive drug, and that once he experienced the high, he wouldn't want to quit.

"So you going to hit this weed or not?" Arab asked in between puffs.

"Yeah, I'll hit it," he said taking the blunt from Arab's hand and putting it to his lips. He took a long drag on the blunt and as soon as the smoke was in his lung, he began to cough.

"You aiirght?" Arab asked patting him on the back.

"I'm cool, cuz," he replied trying to regain his composure.

"I thought I was going to have to call the paramedics or something," Arab said laughing.

"Nah, it ain't that serious," Li'l Loc said passing the blunt back.

They sat and smoked about seven blunts before Arab began searching around the living room.

Li'l Loc thought that Arab was tripping from the weed and he began to laugh. "What the fuck is you doing, cuz?"

"Looking for Blue's keys. I know I seen him put them on the table." After about thirty seconds of searching he found them. "Jackpot!" he said holding them up for Li'l Loc to see.

"What we going to do with them?"

"Let's ride," Arab said picking his gun up from the couch.

Li'l Loc got up off the couch as well and slung his AK over his shoulder. "Where we riding to?"

"You scared or something?" Arab asked tucking his gun into his waistband.

"What you think?"

"Aiight, let's roll then," Arab said leaving the house with Li'l Loc following.

When they got into the car, Arab began adjusting his seat and fixing the mirrors to his liking.

"You sure you know how to drive?" Li'l Loc asked giving him a suspicious look.

"I got this," Arab said starting the car up.

When he pulled off, Li'l Loc turned the music up and relaxed, putting his fate in Arab's hands. He was feeling a little groggy from the after effects of the weed, and after about five minutes of driving, he dozed off in the passenger seat.

Thirty minutes later he felt Arab shaking him, telling him to wake up.

"Where the fuck we at?" he asked looking around.

"The Strip District," Arab replied passing him a freshly-lit dutchee.

"What we doing down here?" Li'l Loc asked taking a hit of the blunt.

"Look over there," Arab replied pointing a few cars over from where they were parked.

"That look like the nigga Wicked's car."

"Yeah, that's his shit."

"So what we going to do?"

"As soon as he come out, we going to spank his bitch ass."

"Right in front of the club?"

"Nah, we going to follow him and catch his ass in traffic," Arab said pulling his gun out and setting it on his lap.

They passed the blunt back and forth as they patiently waited for Wicked to exit the club.

About ten blunts and two hours later, Wicked came walking out with one of his homies.

"There that bitch-ass nigga go right there," Li'l Loc said cocking his AK back.

They watched him as he got in his car, and when he pulled off they followed him close behind. Both of them were quiet, anticipating the work they were about to put in.

Wicked and his homie were oblivious of what was about to happen to them. All the bottles they popped in the club must have been dulling their senses because they didn't see Arab tailing close behind them on the almost empty streets.

Wicked stopped at a light at the corner of Black and Negley Avenue in East Liberty and Arab pulled up behind him. It must have been this nigga's time to die because there wasn't a single could-be witness on the street.

Li'l Loc knew that it was the perfect time, so he began to roll his window down. "Pull on the side of them," he said lifting his AK into firing position.

Arab swerved from behind Wicked's car to the side of them, and before Wicked could duck or pull off, the gunfire erupted.

Kack...kack...kack was the sound of the AK tearing into Wicked and his homie's bodies, leaving them with no chance of survival. When Arab saw that there was no movement in the car, he peeled off leaving nothing but gun smoke and shells at the scene.

They rode through Highland Park and hit the Larimer Bridge on their way back to Homewood. As they drove down Larimer, Arab spotted one of Wicked's homies standing on the corner. He knew that the nigga was a Larimer Avenue hood by the black bandana hanging out of his pocket. As they passed him by, Arab stuck his nine out the window and began shooting. *Boom...boom...boom.*

The shots caught Li'l Loc off guard and he ducked down, thinking they were being shot at.

"I know I hit that nigga," Arab said hitting the gas.

"Hit who?" Li'l Loc asked sitting up in his seat.

"One of them Larimer Avenue niggas," he replied setting the smoking gun on his lap.

"May he die slow," Li'l Loc said turning the music up.

They rode the rest of the way to Li'l Locs house in silence, both of them zoned out to the lyrics coming through the stereo . . . .

CHAPTER 14

Pretty Boy cooked all the coke up by twelve o'clock and he and Bay Boe started bagging up right after. They decided to only bag up one of the keys and stash the rest of the work at LK's house.

By the time school let out, they were halfway through with bagging up and the money was already starting to flow. When Snype and Mr. Boo came through the door, they began to help so they could speed things up. LK and Bundy came through a short while later and they all put their hands to work putting the coke in the Gladlocks.

Together they finished bagging the brick up. They were putting them in bundles of a hundred when someone knocked on the door.

"Damn, the money coming already," Snype said looking at the surveillance monitors. He saw that it was Ki-Ki at the door and he opened it. "What up, Ki-Ki? What you doing here?"

"Pretty Boy told me to come here when school let out."

"Come in," he said walking her into the dining room.

Everybody was hard at work when they entered the room.

"What you doing here?" Bay Boe asked looking up from the table.

"I'm here for Pretty Boy."

"What up, sexy?" he asked as she watched them bag up.

"I though we was going to chill."

"Here I come right now," he said getting up from the table.

"What happened to business first?" Snype asked smiling.

"I'm coming right back," he replied leaving the house.

"So where we going?"

"First I got to go check on my grams, then we can go to the park and kick it for a while."

They stopped at Grams' house and he went in to let her know that he was home. Then they walked to Cliff Park to talk a little.

"So what's up?" he asked her as they sat on the swings.

"Just thinking about you," she told him with a Kool-Aid smile.

"Just thinking about me, huh? You should be thinking about *us*, because ain't no 'I' in we or no 'me' in us," he said while looking in her eyes.

She was feeling him so much and she was worried about him also. Especially after seeing all the drugs on the table at Bay Boe's house. "Please promise me that you're not going to let anything to happen to you in these streets."

"Don't worry about what I'm doing out here because I got everything under control. Me and my niggas is on top of our game, and if things continue to go how they been going, you won't want for anything."

"All I want is you. I don't need the material things to make me happy."

"You got me, but I want to be able to give you the world and everything in it. I know you don't like living in the hood, so I'm going to do whatever it takes for us to be able to relocate."

"My mom is not going to just let me move with you," she said, liking the idea but not thinking that it was possible.

"In two years we will both be eighteen and nothing will hold us back from being able to do what we want to do."

"I hear you and I hope that things go like you want them because I feel like I want to be with you forever."

"I feel the same way," Pretty Boy said giving her a nice long intimate kiss.

They sat at the playground talking for another hour before he walked her home and went back to Bay Boe's spot.

"I thought you said you was coming right back," Bay Boe said as he walked in the door.

"Come on, dog. I was kickin' it with wifey."

"Wifey, huh. Well you need to get your wifey-having ass on them monitors," Bay Boe said joking with him.

The spot was poppin' all day and they made at least ten stacks before it was time to close shop. While they were putting the left-over bundles in a plastic grocery bag for LK to put in the stash at his crib until the next day, Bundy came over the radio.

"Some crabs just rode through flexin' like they want problems."

"Bay Boe hit the button on his walkie-talkie and replied to Bundy, "If they ride back through, let 'em have it."

"No question," Bundy said breaking the connection.

No sooner than the radios went silent, they began hearing shots. *Kack, kack, kack…*the sound of the one hundred-round AKs tearing into the Crips' car.

"What the fuck is going on?" Pretty Boy asked picking up his walkie-talkie.

"We let them niggas have it," LK said over his radio amidst the sound of heavy breathing.

"Where Bundy at?" Bay Boe asked him.

"I'm on my way to the spot."

"Both of ya'll niggas hurry up and come in before the pigs come."

Seconds later they let Bundy and LK into the spot through the back door. Pretty Boy listened closely to the scanner and relayed everything that the police were saying.

"The police probably going to be out there for a while, so everybody might as well get comfortable," Pretty Boy told them.

"Yeah, that would be the best thing," Boo said watching the cop cars on the monitor as they rode up and down the street.

"So what was the niggas driving?" Bay Boe asked them.

"A blue Monte Carlo on gold Daytons and there was three niggas in the car with blue rags on their faces," LK told them.

"I don't think they knew we was out there, because they kept cruising the block like they were looking for someone to get funky on."

"Them niggas got what they deserved," Bay Boe said hoping that shit wouldn't be too hot for them to open up shop the next day.

"Was the driver a dark-skinned nigga with braids?" Pretty Boy asked.

"Yeah, that sound like him," LK replied.

"You know them niggas?" Mr. Boo asked.

"I know him to see him, but we ain't family or nothing," Pretty Boy said.

"So what's his name?" Bay Boe asked.

"They call him DK or Dog Killer. He from Hilltop out Homewood. I use to see him riding around the hood every day in the same Monte Carlo. That's how I know it was for sure him."

"Well, now niggas know that it ain't sweet to ride through here on that bullshit, and if them niggas come trying to retaliate, then we know where to find them," LK said.

They all nodded their heads in agreement, ready to ride at the drop of a dime.

They had school in the morning, so everybody rolled out once they heard the police on the scanner talking about shift change. Pretty Boy was the last to leave and he let Bay Boe know that he would see him in the morning. Tomorrow would be a new day.

*   *   *   *

"Ya'll niggas need to get the fuck up so we can go bust this move," Blue said interrupting their sweet dreams.

"What move?" Li'l Loc asked wiping the sleep from his eyes.

"I got this nigga who want to buy them pounds at a stack apiece, so if ya'll want to get this money, I suggest ya'll start moving."

"How many is he trying to grab?" Arab asked while putting his shoes on.

"How many you trying to sell?" Blue asked.

"I probably keep a few pounds to smoke, so if he trying to buy thirty then that would be cool," Arab answered.

"What about you, Li'l Loc?"

"I'm with Arab. I'm a-keep a few, but I definitely got thirty to sell."

"Well, put them together because the nigga is waiting for us to swing by his spot."

"Aiight," Arab said getting up from the couch and going to the basement with Li'l Loc to grab their stash of pounds.

After putting them in a garbage bag, they left the house to go handle their business.

"So where we going?" Arab asked as Blue pulled away from the curb.

"To the South Side. The nigga who want the pounds live up Knoxville by the Golden Triangle."

"What's his name and how do you know him?" Li'l Loc asked wanting to know who he was dealing with.

"His name is Grim and I did some time with him down the County a few years ago. He had my back when I got into it with these slob niggas from McKeesport."

"So you don't really know the nigga like that?" Arab said plotting in his head.

"Like I said, I know the nigga from the County. We ain't the best of friends, but I fuck with him enough to not rob him."

It took them forty-five minutes to get to Grim's spot and when they pulled up in front of the house, he came out front to meet them. "What up, cuz?" he said dapping Blue up.

"What up?" Blue said returning the embrace.

Grim dapped up Li'l Loc and Arab as well. He trusted Blue so he didn't even question his li'l homies. "Come in the house so we can handle this business," he told them heading inside.

They all sat down in the living room and Grim got straight to business. "So how many of them pounds do ya'll got for me?" he asked them.

"I got ninety pounds and I need a stack apiece for them," Blue told him.

"A stack a pound sounds good. I can definitely do that," Grim said going upstairs to his bedroom to grab the money.

While Grim was in his room, Arab stood up and walked towards the staircase.

"What's wrong?" Blue asked him.

"I got to use the bathroom," Arab said going up the steps. "Yo, cuz, where the bathroom at?" he asked from the upstairs hallway.

"When you come up the steps, it's the first room on the left," Grim hollered from his bedroom closet where he was taking stacks of money out of his safe.

Arab walked past the bathroom to the sound of Grim's voice. "Yo, cuz, I can't find it," he said standing in the doorway of Grim's bedroom with his nine in his hand.

"It's the first door on the left. You can't miss it," Grim said looking up from the money.

"You know what the fuck it is," Arab said pointing the gun at him.

"Ah, shit," Grim said reaching for the gun in his waistband.

"Nah, nigga," Arab said squeezing the trigger. He let off five rounds into Grim's chest and head before his body hit the ground.

"What the fuck was that?" Blue asked.

"I don't know," Li'l Loc said jumping up from the couch and running up the stairs.

Blue followed close behind him with his gun out and when he got to the bedroom, he was shocked by the sight of Grim lying on the ground with his brains blown out.

"What the fuck you kill him for?" Li'l Loc asked staring at Grim's lifeless body.

"Fuck that nigga. Just help me put this money in the bag," Arab replied.

"I can't believe you killed that nigga," Blue said helping him with the money while Li'l Loc searched the rest of the bedroom.

Li'l Loc went through all the dressers, pocketing every watch chain and ring that he could find. He then looked up and noticed that Grim had a drop ceiling. He got on top of the bed and gave the ceiling a push. Two keys of cocaine fell right into his hands. "Jackpot!" he said with a smile on his face.

When they were done putting the money in the bag, they all ran down the steps and out the house.

"What the fuck is you thinking?" Blue said as they all got into the car.

"You said ya'll wasn't the best of friends," Arab said smiling at the success of their robbery.

"Fuck it now. We got the money and that's all that matter," Li'l Loc said reminding Blue that it was money over everything.

Blue knew that Li'l Loc was right, and he couldn't be mad because this was the code that he always lived by. He looked over at Arab and shook his head. In his heart he knew that he would have to kill him for going against his word, but he would save that for a later day.

"How much money do you think we got?" Li'l Loc asked from the back seat.

"It got to be at least two hundred, fifty thousand," Arab said looking in the bag sitting on the floor between his legs.

"We got to get rid of this car as soon as possible and you got to get rid of that gun," Blue told Arab.

"I know, cuz," Arab said turning the music up to block out the sound of Blue's voice. He knew that Blue was mad at him for killing Grim, but he didn't give a fuck. The simple fact was, Grim wasn't from their hood and the money was just too much to pass up.

They got back to the hood in about twenty minutes, which was half the time it took to get to Grim's spot. The whole way home, Blue was praying that the jakes didn't jump on him, because the last thing he wanted to do was get caught in his ride with a murder weapon.

After parking in front of Li'l Loc's house, they all got out of the car and went inside.

"Let's count this change up," Arab said setting the bag in the middle of the floor.

"And we got to weigh this coke up," Li'l Loc said pulling the two keys out from inside his coat.

It took them about thirty minutes to count all the money. It was less than they thought, but the coke weighed exactly seventy-two ounces.

"One hundred, thirty thousand dollars. So that means we get forty-three thousand apiece with a little left over to grab some new guns," Blue told them.

Li'l Loc and Arab smiled at each other. They were now on their way to being them niggas and they felt like nothing could stop them.

Arab didn't feel sorry for killing Grim. In fact, he felt that Grim deserved to get killed for slipping so hard.

"I'm a-go take my ride to the chop shop and when I get back we going to go grab some new toast," Blue told them before leaving the house.

When Blue was gone, Arab spoke up, "Yo, cuz, you think he mad at me for killing Grim?"

"Fuck Grim. That nigga shouldn't have been slipping," Li'l Loc replied.

"I was thinking the same thing."

"So what we going to do with this work?" Li'l Loc asked him. He didn't have any experience in hustling, and he didn't really want to get caught up in the hustling side of things.

"The nigga Blue probably got something up his sleeve for us. But if worst come to worst, then we going to have to move it on our own."

"I was hoping it didn't come to that," Li'l Loc replied.

"I feel the same way," Arab said, splitting out one of his dutchees so he could roll up some of the weed he had.

Three hours and a bunch of blunts later, Blue woke them up with two guns in his hands.

"What the fuck is you doing, cuz?" Li'l Loc said sitting upon the couch.

"I just grabbed these three mini Mac elevens from my gun connect," he said handing them each a gun with two extra thirty-shot clips.

"So what should I do with my nine?" Arab said pulling the gun from his waist.

"Hand it here and I'll get rid of it. Also I'm going to sell the pounds and the coke to this one nigga I fuck with."

"So when we going to holler at him?" Li'l Loc asked.

"I'm a-handle it by myself," Blue said not wanting a repeat of what happened with Grim.

"What, you don't trust us, cuz?" Arab asked.

"Yeah, I trust you, but it's the greed inside of you that I got a problem with," Blue said smiling at him.

"So when is you going to holler at him?" Li'l Loc asked.

"I just talked to the nigga a hour ago and he said that he ready whenever."

"How much money is he going to give us for everything?" Arab asked.

"He going to give us twenty-four thousand apiece for the birds and he going to give us eight hundred dollars a pound," Blue told them, throwing in his cut that he was going to take out of the thousand that his man paid for each pound.

"Let's get it cracking then," Li'l Loc said wanting to turn the drugs into cash in a hurry.

"I'm a-just wait until daylight because I don't know if the police is hot on us for the shit we done."

"So what we going to do until then?" Arab asked.

"First I'm going to go get rid of this hot gun, then I'm going to go upstairs and kick it with my woman until the A.M. Ya'll niggas just sit tight and stay out of trouble," he told them seriously.

Right after Blue left, Arab picked up the phone and started dialing.

"Who you calling?"

"Sharell and Tamika from up Hilltop," Arab said.

"What you calling them hoes for?"

"I seen the broad Tamika the other day and she said that she want to holler at you," Arab told him.

"So you be fucking with Sharell?" Li'l Loc asked him.

"I smutted her a few times, but I don't fuck with her," Arab said. He was a hoe magnet and it was nothing for him to smut out hoes on a regular basis. Li'l Loc, on the other hand, was a little shy when it came to the hoes, but he had seen Tamika around and he was definitely interested in her.

Sharell answered on the fifth ring and Arab smiled and nodded his head to let Li'l Lock know that it was on.

"Who this?" she asked him.

"It's your man, Arab," he said flirtatiously.

"What up, Arab? What you doing?" she asked him.

"I'm down Li'l Loc's house and he trying to get at your friend Tamika."

"Hold on," she told him putting the phone down.

He could hear her voice in the background, but he couldn't make out what she was saying.

She had him on hold for a minute or two before getting back on the phone. "Tamika said she don't know who Li'l Loc is."

"She know who CJ is, right?"

"Yeah, we know cute-ass CJ."

"Well, we call him Li'l Loc now," Arab explained to her.

"So ya'll want us to come over his house?" she asked.

"If ya'll want to come through."

"We on our way right now," she told him before hanging the phone up.

Arab rolled a few blunts up as they waited for their hook-ups to come. It took the girls about an hour to get to Li'l Loc's house, and Arab snapped on them for taking so long as soon as they walked through the door.

"What the fuck was the hold up?" he asked Sharell, who sat down on the couch next to him.

"We had to get dressed and after that it was hard to get a jitney," Sharell told him defensively.

"So what's up, Li'l Loc?" Tamika said sitting down next to him.

"Ain't shit, just relaxin' like always" he said a little withdrawn.

"Why you acting all shy?" Sharell said laughing.

"He ain't shy . . . he just chillin," Arab said picking up a blunt from the table and firing it up. He took a few puffs and passed it to Li'l Loc.

"Damn, I thought you was a good boy. Now you smoking weed and shit," Tamika said smiling at him.

"Well, I ain't the same old CJ no more," he replied taking a long drag of the dutchee.

"Ain't nothing wrong with that. Anyway, I like gangstas," Tamika told him.

"Is that right?" he asked while passing her the blunt.

"That's right," she said in a sexy tone as she took a hit of the weed.

He knew by her tone that she was down for whatever, so he took her by the hand and led her upstairs to his bedroom. The room was more like a storage room, which was why he slept in the living room on the couch. All that he had in the bedroom was an old mattress in the middle of the floor surrounded by boxes of shit they never used.

"So what you bring me up here for?"

"Lay down on the bed so I can show you," he told her.

She did as she was told and he sat on the mattress right beside her and took his shirt off.

"Damn," she said looking at his muscular form. His physique had her pussy juices dripping and she felt like she was about to explode.

"So you like what you see?" he asked pulling her shirt over her head.

"Hell, yeah," she replied kicking her shoes off.

As he took her pants off, she took her bra off and tossed it on the floor. When he looked at her body he was speechless. In his eyes, she was a bad bitch and he knew that he was about to beat her little pussy out the frame.

"What you waiting for?" she asked interrupting his thoughts.

"Slow down, sexy," he said taking his pants off. When he was completely undressed, he got on top of her and slid his manhood inside of her. "Damn, you got some wet wet," he said fucking her nice and slow.

"You like this pussy, CJ?" she asked in between moans.

"Call me Li'l Loc," he said fucking her harder.

"Aiight, Li'l Loc!" she screamed loving the way he was beating down her walls.

He fucked her harder and harder as she screamed out. "Fuck me, Li'l Loc…oohh…please don't stop!" Over and over.

"Turn over," he told her in an aggressive tone, his thug passion turning her on even more.

"Beat this pussy up!" she screamed while throwing it back at him, meeting him thrust for thrust. It didn't take long for her to come all over his dick, but she wasn't finished with him.

"Lay on your back so I can ride that dick," she said, shaking from the orgasm that she had.

He laid on his back and she jumped on top of his dick, riding him like a professional porno star.

"You like the way I'm working this pussy, don't you?" she asked while sliding up and down his pole.

"Yeah, you twirkin' it," he said grabbing on to her ass so he could match her rhythm.

"I'm about to come, CJ," she said riding him harder and faster.

"Bitch, my name is Li'l Loc," he said pounding his dick inside of her, not too far from busting a nut of his own.

The way he talked to her threw her over the edge and she screamed, "Come with me, Li'l Loc," as the orgasm hit, causing her to come all over his dick.

Her pussy was so good that he couldn't hold back any longer. He clinched her ass tight and rammed his dick inside of her and busted off.

He didn't even think of whether not she was on birth control or anything, and she didn't think to ask him to put a condom on. They were both caught up in the moment and they felt that if anything came of it, then so be it.

They were both lying in bed, spent from the bomb sex session, thinking about going at it again once they were ready, when Arab knocked on the door interrupting them.

"Who that?" Li'l Loc asked too tired to get up from the bed.

"Yo, cuz, I need to holler at you," Arab said from the hallway.

"I'll be right back," Li'l Loc said putting on his clothes and going to the door.

"What ya'll doing in there?" Arab asked as he walked out into the hallway.

"Nigga, what you think?" Li'l Loc replied smiling.

"That's what I'm talking about, nigga," Arab said dapping him up.

"So what you want?" Li'l Loc asked ready to go back in the room for round two.

"Oh, yeah," Arab said remembering why he came upstairs. "Sharell's mom said they got to get back to the house."

"What that got to do with Tamika?"

"She supposed to be spending the night at Sharell's house so she got to leave with her," Arab told him spoiling his plans for another shot of pussy.

"I'm a-tell her to get dressed," Li'l Loc said going back into the bedroom.

"What did he want?"

"He said that Sharell's mom called and ya'll got to roll out."

"Damn, I thought we was going to have a round two," she said reading his mind.

"We can hook up some other time."

"I'm definitely with that," she said getting dressed.

After she got dressed, he walked her downstairs and they all sat in the living room while waiting for the jitney they called to come pick them up.

"So did ya'll have fun?" Sharell asked throwing her hair in a pony tail.

"It was aiight," Li'l Loc replied nonchalantly.

"It was more than aiight," Tamika said smiling. She wished that she could stay so she could get her back blown out some more.

But she knew that she would have hell to pay if Sharell's mom told her mom that she was out all night.

It took about twenty minutes for their jitney to come. Both of them got up to leave when they heard the car beeping the horn in front of the house.

"So ya'll going to call us tomorrow, right?" Sharell asked before leaving.

"Maybe," Arab said smiling. Sharell was just a hit to him and she definitely didn't have top priority in his life.

"Well, I don't know about you, Arab, but I know that Li'l Loc better call me or I'm going to come looking for him," Tamika said smiling.

"I'm a-call you," Li'l Loc said ushering them out the door.

As soon as they got in their jitney, Blue hoped out of his ride. After paying his own personal jitney, he walked in the house. "Who was that leaving from here?" he asked sitting on the couch.

"Just some smuts," Arab said with a smirk on his face.

"Fuck them though. Did you get rid of that strap?" Li'l Loc asked changing the subject. He was feeling Tamika a little bit and even though he knew she was out there, he wasn't trying to talk about what he did with her.

"Yeah, I handled that. And I bumped into one of the locs around the corner."

"Who you talking about?" Arab asked wondering what he was getting at.

"The nigga told me that Wicked got hit with a AK on the corner of Black and Negley. Ya'll wouldn't happen to know anything about that?" he asked them.

"Why would we know something about that? And we been with you all day," Li'l Loc told him.

"Well, the nigga—whose name I won't say—said he seen ya'll in my car down the Strip, and he also said that when Wicked left the club, ya'll followed him."

"Like I said, we don't know nothing about that, so whoever told you that must be mistaken," Arab told him.

"I'm not saying that I don't believe ya'll, but I'm a-need that AK so I can get rid of it for ya'll just in case ya'll not being up front with me."

"Aiight," Li'l Loc said going down to the basement to grab the gun.

He and Arab hated to have to lie to Blue, but they didn't want him to know that they took his car and put some work in out of it without his approval. It was bad enough that Arab killed his man Grim, and they could both tell that Blue felt some type of way about it, even though he didn't say anything.

When Li'l Loc came back upstairs with the gun, Blue wrapped it in a garbage bag and called another ride. When his ride came, he left the house telling them once again to stay in for the night and not to get into any more shit.

After Blue left, they smoked about four more blunts and talked about what they were going to do with all their money until they both nodded off.

CHAPTER 15

*K*nock, knock, knock was the sound that woke Pretty Boy from his sleep. He reached under his mattress and grabbed his thirty-shot Glock forty before going to answer the door.

It seemed like he became more and more paranoid everyday. He and his homies had been slanging hard for the past two months and he knew that sooner or later niggas would be trying their nuts.

They conducted their business just as they said they would: breaking keys down and selling them from Bay Boe's house and making the most money they could from beating up the block. They did this for a month straight, and by the end of the month they were buying three birds and getting three on consignment.

When the second month came, they began selling weight to the hustlers in the hood to take the heat off of themselves. This worked to their advantage because they didn't have to spend as much time bagging up. Also, their hustle didn't interfere with the last month of school. Now that it was summer vacation, they could really get their hustle on twenty-four seven.

"Who is it at the door?" Grams hollered from her room. The loud knocking must have awaken her from her sleep.

"I don't know yet," he replied loud enough for her to hear, but trying not to holler. When he got to the door, he peeped through the peep hole and saw that it was his homie Bay-Boe.

"What up?" he asked opening the door to let him in.

"Get dressed and come on," Bay Boe said seriously.

"It's three in the morning. Can't this wait?" he asked, wiping the sleep from his eyes.

"Just come on," Bay Boe said sitting down on the living room couch.

Pretty Boy knew that it had to be serous, so he went back to his room to get dressed. He threw on that all-black attire: black Dickies, black Timbs and a black hoodie on top of his black t-shirt. Before leaving his room, he hung his red rag from his back pocket and then went back downstairs to see what was up with his homie.

"Let's go," Bay Boe said getting up from the couch and leaving the house with Pretty Boy close behind.

When they arrived at Bay Boe's house, he saw that everybody was in the living room looking around as if they were lost.

"So what's up?" he asked.

Bay Boe pointed at Snype, who was sitting on the couch with his arm in a sling.

"What the fuck happened to you?"

"I was going to my crib to make a drop-off when the nigga with the blue MC that we shot at pulled up beside me and started letting off. I let off a few shots to get them off my ass, but I took one in the shoulder before they sped off."

"We need you to show us where the niggas be at," Bay Boe told him.

"No question," Pretty Boy replied ready to ride for his homies.

"We got LK out trying to steal us a mini van. He should be back any minute and then we going to ride out," Mr. Boo told him.

Pretty Boy sat down on the couch and poured himself a cup of the Hennessy that was on the table. He downed the drink in two sips and then took a hit of the blunt that Bay Boe passed him. The liquor and weed erased any fears of putting in work. Five minutes later LK came walking into the house.

"Ya'll ready to ride?" he asked picking up his AK from the table.

"Hell, yeah," they all replied leaving the house.

LK had stolen an all-black mini van that had automatic sliding doors on both sides. LK was driving and the rest of the homies were in the back smoking weed and checking their guns to make sure that they were ready.

They were listening to a song from a local group's album called the Sinate, and the words *Where the fuck are you from* being repeated over and over had them ready to ride for their hood and let the Hilltop niggas know that they weren't pussy.

Pretty Boy gave LK directions and prayed to himself that they didn't get pulled over. They drove for about a half hour before entering Homewood.

Once in the neighborhood, they all put their red bandanas over their faces. They weren't worried about anybody seeing their faces because the van's rear windows were fully tinted. LK drove for another ten minutes after entering Homewood before Pretty Boy told him to pull over.

"What up?" Bay Boe asked him.

"Them projects at the top of the hill is Hilltop. It's only one way in and one way out, so we going to have to be shooting from the time we enter to the time we leave."

"Hit the doors," Bundy told LK ready to get it poppin'.

When the sliding doors were open, LK shut the lights off and hit the gas. They entered into the projects and saw the blue Monte Carlo on the gold D's parked in front of a house with a few Crips sitting on the hood not paying any attention.

It was at this time that the gunfire erupted from the van. They were shooting from both sides of the van, trying to hit any and everything in sight.

TAT...TAT...TAT...BOOM...BOOM...BOOM was all that was heard as the Crips attempted to take cover. Bullets ripped through them as well as through house windows, cars and anybody outside. A few people shot back, but were no match for the gunfire coming from the van.

As they exited the projects, LK shut both of the sliding doors and began driving at a regular pace so they wouldn't look suspicious. Everyone was silent on the way back to the Hill District, and every time they saw a police car they grew tense and paranoid, not wanting to get knocked.

When they pulled up in front of Bay Boe's house, everybody hopped out of the van.

"Make sure you burn this muthafucka," Bay Boe told LK as he went up the steps to his house.

"No question," he replied pulling off to handle his business.

When they were safe inside the house, everyone began to drink and smoke, trying to ease the tension and paranoia of what they had just done.

"That's how you ride," Bay Boe said loosening up from the effects of the weed and alcohol. "Ain't no way them niggas is alive."

"We chopped them niggas the fuck up," Mr. Boo said wiping the guns down with his bandana.

A half hour later, LK came walking back into the house, throwing up a CK for Crip Killer with both hands before sitting down to pour himself a drink.

Mr. Boo put all the clean guns in a bag and gave them to Bundy to get rid of. "Bury them in the woods," he told him.

"I got it," Bundy replied before leaving.

"Now we need some more guns," Pretty Boy said feeling naked without his Glock.

"As soon as the morning hit, we going to hit. We going to call CK Black being as though we need to re-up anyway," Bay Boe said.

The last time they copped, they bought five birds and got five birds on consignment. The birds were gone in two weeks and they were ready for more. They averaged about twenty-eight thousand dollars a key selling some niggas soft and some niggas hard. Off of ten birds they made two hundred and eighty thousand, making an eighty thousand dollar profit.

They each took home ten thousand and they planned to use the other two hundred and twenty thousand to buy six birds and get six on consignment, with the hundred thousand they owed CK Black included in the two hundred and twenty thousand.

"Ya'll should have at least eighty thousand put up from them other flips, so everybody just pitch in five thousand apiece towards the guns," Bay Boe told them.

Everybody agreed on putting up five grand because they knew that they would need more guns than they had before.

After a few more drinks and blunts everyone began to stagger home. Pretty Boy was the last to leave and when he got up from the couch, Bay Boe got up as well. He dapped Pretty Boy up and looked him in the eyes.

"You know that I would die for you, right?" Bay Boe told him.

"I would do the same for you," Pretty Boy replied with sincerity in his voice. He knew that he would definitely take a bullet for his homie if it ever came down to it, and he would kill for his homie as well.

"As long as you know," Bay Boe said staggering back to the couch where he laid down and passed out.

Pretty Boy left the house and locked the door behind him. He headed home in a rush, trying not to be caught slipping without his strap.

He was so twisted that he skipped right pass his grams' room. He went straight to his room, pulled his shoe box out from beneath his bed and began to count his profits from the last two months. He had a little over eighty thousand dollars in the stash. He took out the five thousand that he would need to pitch in for guns.

He didn't spend large sums of his hard-earned money and neither did any of his homies. They had even cut down on their weed habit. Pretty Boy's goal was to stack a quarter million before he turned eighteen, and by the look of it, he would get there a hell of a lot quicker.

He had also promised Ki-Ki that he would buy them a house in the suburbs. She didn't really believe him, but he knew that it was possible with all the money they were getting. As he laid back on the bed thinking of his future, the sun shining through the window interrupted his thoughts. He turned to the clock to see what time it was and was surprised. *Damn, it's six o'clock*, he said to himself. He threw the blanket over his head and five minutes later he was out cold.

*   *   *   *

"Brandon, wake up! There's someone at the door!" Grams hollered from the bottom of the steps.

He looked over at the clock which read 9:00 A.M. "Damn, I just went to sleep," he said getting up. He was feeling like shit and he didn't really want to be bothered, but he knew he had to get up to go see who was at the door.

When he got downstairs, the door was cracked and he could see Ki-Ki standing in front of his house. He perked up at the sight of her. "What you doing up this early?" he asked letting her in the house.

"I was thinking about you all night and I wanted to see what you was doing, so here I am."

He led her into the kitchen where his grams was cooking and introduced them to each other.

"Grams, this is my girl Quiana…Quiana, this is my grams."

"Good morning, baby," Grams said looking her up and down. She seemed like a nice girl, so Grams nodded her head in approval. "You hungry?" Grams asked while setting a plate in front of her.

"Do I have a choice?" Ki-Ki asked smiling.

"Not really," Grams replied giggling as she sat another plate in front of Pretty Boy.

While they were eating, Grams went to her room to get dressed. Twenty minutes later she came back downstairs and into the dining room. "I'm a-leave ya'll two alone because I have to run downtown to grab a few things. I probably won't be back for a few hours, so lock up the house if you leave," she told him.

"It was nice meeting you, Grams," Ki-Ki told her.

"Nice meeting you, too," Grams replied before leaving.

"Your grams is nice," Ki-Ki said eating her breakfast.

"Yeah, she cool," he replied in between bites. He still felt a little hung over from the night before and his head was throbbing, so he spoke very little while eating.

"Why you so quiet, baby?" Ki-Ki asked him.

"Just a little tired," he said getting up to wash his plate off.

"If you want me to come back later, I can go," she said handing him her plate to wash also.

"You don't got to leave," he said drying off the dishes and setting them back into the cabinet. When he was done, he took her by the hand and led her upstairs to his room.

"You got a nice bedroom," she said liking the way everything was set up.

"Thanks," he replied taking his shirt off so he could hop in the shower before getting dressed.

Seeing him with his shirt off made her blush and look away.

"What's wrong?" he asked after seeing her turn away from him.

"Ain't nothing wrong. It's just you are so sexy with your shirt off."

"So you like what you see?" he asked sitting down on the bed next to her.

"Yes, I like it," she replied touching his bare chest. The feel of his muscles against her hand had her tingling inside and her pussy began to throb. The sexual tension that she felt was too much to control and she leaned in to kiss him.

Feeling her soft lips on his had his manhood at attention and he went up her shirt to unhook her bra so he could caress her hard nipples. But before he could get her bra off, she pulled back.

"Wait, baby," she said breaking their embrace.

"What's wrong?" he asked leaning in to kiss her on the neck.

"I never did this before, and if it is going to happen then I need to know that you really care about me."

When he heard her say this, he stopped kissing her on the neck and looked in her eyes. "I don't just care about you...I love you."

She looked in his eyes for any sign that he was lying, but all she saw was sincerity and honest, so she moved closer and began to kiss him again.

In between kisses they both undressed, and when he had her completely naked, he sat there and admired her banging body. "You are perfect," he said causing her to smile and pull him in for a kiss.

Since she was a virgin it was hard for him to enter her, but once he did it was the best feeling in the world. He took it nice and slow, working himself in and out of her wetness at a slow pace so not to hurt her. Her eyes were closed and her arms were wrapped around him tight. While he was making love to her, she was whispering "I love you" in his ear over and over again as her pain turned into pleasure.

They made love for thirty minutes and she was about to come for the third time. "Come with me, baby," she said in between moans.

He began to thrust himself in and out of her harder and faster until they came together. When they were finished they laid in bed and held each other, neither one of them wanting to be the first to let go. The sound of someone knocking on the door interrupted their moment and both of them were mad that it had to end.

"I wonder who that could be?" he said while putting his clothes on. After getting dressed, he went to answer the door and cautiously looked out the peephole. Seeing that it was his homie Bay Boe, he opened the door and let him in. "What up, Ikey?" he asked dapping him up.

"You know what's up. I just talked to CK Black and he said that he ready for us."

"I'm a-go hop in the shower and get dressed first. Is you hungry?" he asked Bay Boe before going back up the stairs.

"I'm hungry and hung over," Bay Boe replied.

"I was feeling the same way when I woke up and my grams' cooking will definitely have you feeling better, or at least it worked for me. Anyway, the food is on the stove. Grab a plate and put you something together," he said gong to his room.

"What was that?" Ki-Ki asked when he walked back in the room.

"Me and Bay Boe suppose to go handle some business," he said while getting ready to hop in the shower.

"So when you going to have some more time for me?" she asked putting her clothes on.

"Just be patient and soon you will have all my time," he said thinking about his plans for them.

"I am patient," she said following his lead.

"When I get out the shower, I'll walk you to the door," he said leaving the room.

Once he was gone, she began searching through his room. She went through all the dresser drawers looking for any evidence that would show she was not the only female in his life. After searching through everything, she was satisfied that she was his one and only, but something told her to keep looking.

As she continued to search, something directed her attention to the shoe box under his bed. She reached under the bed and pulled the box out. When she opened it, she gasped at what she saw inside. The box was filled with money and most of it was hundred dollar bills. She had never seen so much money in her life and she wondered how much it was. Before she could attempt to count it, she heard the shower stop.

She quickly put the money back under the bed where she found it and, about two minutes later, Pretty Boy came walking back into the room. She watched him as he got dressed, realizing that he wasn't the same Brandon that she met a few months ago. Now he was a big-time drug dealer and even though she didn't want to be involved with one before, the money in the box had her rethinking her position. In fact, she was intoxicated by it.

"You ready to go?" he asked interrupting her thoughts.

"Not really," she said smiling.

"Me either, but I got to go make moves, so come on," he said leading her downstairs.

On his way to the front door, he stopped in the kitchen to make sure Bay Boe was aiight.

"What up, Bay Boe?" she asked seeing him at the kitchen table.

He looked up from his second plate of food and smiled. "The question is, what's up with you?"

"Just chilling with my man," she replied with a Kool-Aid smile on her face.

"You sure that's all you were doing?"

Before she could reply, Pretty Boy intervened. "Come on," he said walking her to the door. He gave her a kiss before she left and watched her thick hips sway back and forth as she walked away.

Bay Boe grilled him as soon as he walked back into the kitchen. "Damn, Ikey, you hit that?" he asked.

"A real gentleman never tells," he replied.

"You a cold nigga," Bay Boe told him reading into the saying.

"Fuck all that, though. What's up with CK Black and them guns?" Pretty Boy asked changing the subject.

"He say he got a bunch of shit for us so we cool on that tip."

"Let's head to your house then, so we can put the money together," Pretty Boy said following him out of the house. After making sure the door was locked, they headed around the corner to Bay Boe's house. Once inside his room, they began to count all the money up.

After two hours of counting it over and over again to make sure it was straight, they stuffed the money into a book bag.

"I wish I had a gun because I feel more naked than a muthafucka going over there with all this money," Bay Boe said picking up the phone to call their personal jitney, Mr. Ray.

"I feel the same way," Pretty Boy said looking at the bag of money. Even though CK Black never pulled any grimy shit on them in the past, both of them still wanted to be prepared just in case.

Mr. Ray didn't answer the phone the first time, so they decided to wait a few minutes before trying again.

"Damn, I forgot to put the money for the guns in with the flip," Bay Boe said going back to the safe to grab an extra thirty thousand dollars.

"I left my five stacks at the spot, but I can go get it if you need me to," Pretty Boy told him.

"It's gravy . . . just grab it when we get back. I got to put the money in for everybody else until they get here anyway," he said counting the money to make sure it was straight.

As soon as he was done, LK and Snype walked into the room.

"What it be like?" Pretty Boy said dapping them both up.

"Ya'll see the news this morning?" Snype asked turning on the television to show them what he was talking about.

"Hell, nah. I was hung the fuck over trying to sleep off that Hennessy we drunk last night," Bay Boe replied.

"I was fucked up, too," Pretty Boy said shaking his head.

Snype turned to the twenty-four hour local news station to see if he could catch it, but nothing came up. "Well we got three of them niggas and left five others in critical condition."

"What they say about suspects?" Bay Boe asked.

"Ain't nobody talking on their side, so we good on that note," Snype answered.

"We definitely going to need them guns because I know them niggas is going to retaliate," Pretty Boy said of the Hilltop niggas' reputation for putting in work.

As soon as Bay Boe was about to try to call Mr. Ray again, the phone rang. "Who this?" he said answering the phone.

"Somebody call a jitney from this number?"

"This is Bay Boe from Roberts Street, and I'm trying to make a run out Garfield."

"I'm on my way," Mr. Ray said knowing that they always paid him good money to make trips.

"Anybody know where Bundy and Mr. Boo at?" Pretty Boy asked.

"I talked to both of them niggas earlier and they both sounded fucked up from last night, but they said they were on their way," LK answered.

"How long ago was this?" Bay Boe asked him.

"About an hour ago," LK replied.

Before they could continue their conversation, they heard the jitney out front beeping the horn.

"Let's go handle this business," Bay Boe told Pretty Boy.

"Ya'll just sit tight, and if anybody come looking for work, tell them we on our way," Pretty Boy said leaving the house behind Bay Boe.

After getting into the jitney and greeting Mr. Ray, they both tried to relax. This was practically impossible, though, without their guns on them. Even though they seemed cool, their paranoia was ten times worse than any other time they went to re-up. Not only did they not have their guns, they were carrying a quarter million in a book bag, which didn't help the situation at all.

When they entered the Columbo projects, their paranoia increased. Pretty Boy reached for his gun by instinct only to come up empty handed. There were even more people out and they all looked like they were in defense mode.

Mr. Ray pulled over in front of the house he always took them to and turned the car off. Bay Boe hopped out of the car clutching the bag full of money as they headed to CK Black's spot, dapping up a few of the Bloods on their way.

CK Black opened the door before they could even knock. "What up, Blood?" he said letting them in the house.

"What up, Ike?" they both replied going inside.

When they got to the dining room they noticed an arsenal of guns on the table. There were assault rifles, handguns, machine guns and revolvers. Also he had ten bullet-proof vests sitting on the table.

All in all, there were twenty AKs, fifteen Glocks, twenty revolvers, five TEC-9s, five MAC-10s and ten Calicos. Included with the guns were extended clips and boxes on top of boxes of ammo.

"This is a lot of shit," Bay Boe said looking at all the guns.

"Just know that ya'll going to be aiight on guns for a long time," CK Black replied smiling at the look on their faces.

"Load them up in these two duffle bags. Also, how many birds ya'll trying to grab?

"We need seven," Bay Boe told him.

"No problem," he said leaving the room to go get the work.

As soon as they were done loading all the guns into the duffle bags, CK came back in the room with another duffle bag and set it on the table for them to inspect.

Pretty Boy looked into the bag and counted out fourteen birds. Satisfied with what he saw, he then zipped the bag up and sat it next to the bag of guns.

"Ya'll hear about them crabs getting killed up Hilltop?" CK asked wondering if that was the reason they needed the guns.

"We seen it on the news this morning, but we don't know too much about what happened," Bay Boe said grinning.

"So ya'll good then?" CK said dapping them up.

"Yeah, we good," they both replied as he walked them to the door.

Before they left, Bay Boe commented on all the extra people outside.

"You noticed that, huh?" CK replied.

"Hell, yeah, we noticed it," Pretty Boy said.

"Some nigga name Wicked from Larimer got killed a short while ago about three blocks from here. His homies think we had something to do with it, so we on point just in case they try something."

"Do you know who did it?" Bay Boe asked.

"I know that it wasn't any of my homies, and word on the streets is some young nigga from Homewood may have did him."

"What's the nigga's name?" Pretty Boy asked thinking that maybe he would know him.

"From what I hear, they call him Li'l Loc and he robbed Wicked not too long ago. I just figured that he finished the job before Wicked could finish him," he explained before they left.

C.K Black knew that they probably had something to do with the murders up Hilltop whether they wanted to admit it or not. The grin that Bay Boe gave him when he asked said it all. He just hoped nothing bad happened to his little homies because he really liked them.

They walked back to the jitney and signaled for him to pop the trunk. After putting the guns and drugs inside, they got in the car.

"Drive the speed limit and be careful," Bay Boe said handing him two hundred dollar bills.

They knew that if they got busted with all the guns and drugs they were carrying, they would both be charged as adults and that was something they were trying to avoid, especially with all the money they were now making.

Lady Luck was on their side and they made it to Bay Boe's house safe and sound. They both hopped out of the car and went to the trunk. After grabbing the work and guns, they went into the house.

Bundy and Mr. Boo had come through right after they left and were now sitting in the living room with the rest of their crew.

"Ya'll get the guns?" Snype asked massaging his wounded shoulder.

"We got the guns and work," Pretty Boy said unzipping the duffle bags for them to see.

"Everybody got their five stacks?" Bay Boe asked.

They all put their money on the table except for Pretty Boy who had to go home to grab his.

After Bay Boe grabbed all the money and put it in his stash, Pretty Boy began taking the birds out of the duffle bag so he could begin whipping some of the coke up.

Looking at all the guns and work made them feel untouchable. At that point, Pretty Boy started to forget his reasons for hustling. He felt like he was on top of his game and he should be shining to show it. In fact, he planned to do that as soon as they moved all the work they had.

He looked around the table at his new family and began nodding his head in pride. He knew that there weren't too many niggas on their level. They were young, they were getting money and everybody on their squad would kill at the drop of a dime.

CHAPTER 16

"Rise and shine, niggas," Blue said entering the living room.

"What the fuck time is it?" Li'l Loc asked.

"It's two in the afternoon," Blue told him.

"Is you sure?" Li'l Loc questioned looking at his iced-out watch.

"Yeah, I'm sure. I should have woke ya'll up earlier because I got to go make that move I told ya'll about."

"You sure you don't want us to roll?" Arab asked.

"Yeah, I'm sure," Blue replied passing him a half-smoked blunt.

"What about this jewelry I got?" Li'l Loc asked pulling the two necklaces, one watch and an iced-out bracelet from his pocket.

"Where the fuck you get this shit from?" Blue asked taking the jewelry from him.

"I got it from the nigga Grim's dresser while ya'll was grabbing the money."

"They might be able to trace this shit to his murder, so I think it will be best to sell it," Blue suggested.

"Fuck that. I want that chain," Arab said not giving a fuck if somebody noticed it or not. The chain was icy as hell and he knew that his pussy rate would go sky high if he had it on his neck.

"Here then, nigga," Blue said tossing him the chain. "If you get knocked wearing it, don't come crying to me."

Arab threw the chain around his neck and got up to check himself out in the mirror while ignoring Blue's comment.

Blue just shook is head at Arab's hot headedness, and he knew that either he would have to do something about it or Arab would be his downfall.

"You want us to go grab them pounds right now?" Li'l Loc asked interrupting his thoughts.

"Yeah, go put that together so I can bust this move, and when I get back, I'll take ya'll to this li'l car lot so we can check out new whips for all of us."

This had Arab and Li'l Loc both hyped-up and in their minds they were already picturing the type of cars they wanted. After grabbing the weed and coke from the basement and giving it to Blue to sell for them, they sat back and conversed over a few blunts.

"So what type of whip you planning on grabbing?" Li'l Loc asked Arab.

"Something new and flashy," Arab replied wanting to stunt for the summer.

"We might as well pitch in and just buy one hot-ass whip, since we be together all the time anyway," Li'l Loc suggested.

"I'm definitely with that," Arab said pulling a shoe box filled with money from under the couch.

"How much money you going to take?" Li'l Loc asked him.

"Around twenty thousand," Arab replied counting it out.

Li'l Loc went in his stash, pulled out his money and counted out the same amount. He knew that whatever type of whip they grabbed for forty thousand would be the nicest thing on the streets.

They sat and smoked blunt after blunt until Blue came back through the door from handling his business.

"Ya'll niggas look zooted," he said sitting down.

"We blew damn near a ounce since you left," Li'l Loc told him.

"I can tell," Blue replied looking at his chinky eyes.

"So what's up with that money?" Arab asked ready to get his cut.

"I almost forgot," Blue said pulling a bag out of his coat filled up with money, mainly hundred dollar bills.

"So he bought everything?" Li'l Loc asked.

"Yeah, he bought everything, including the jewels," Blue replied dumping the knots of money on the table.

"So how much did he pay for everything?" Arab asked.

"He ended up paying a stack a pound, and he bought the two birds for twenty-four thousand dollars apiece."

"What he give us for them jewels?" Li'l Loc asked.

"I just told him to give me six thousand for everything, so from everything we each get forty-eight thousand apiece."

After giving everybody their cut, Blue stood up. "Ya'll ready to hit this car lot?"

"Without a doubt," Li'l Loc said ready to get his shine on.

"So where the car lot at?" Arab asked.

"It's on Route 51, by the old skating rink."

Arab picked up the phone and called a jitney. He got an answer after the second ring, and after giving the jitney directions, he hung up the phone.

When they heard the jitney out front beeping the horn, Li'l Loc and Arab tucked their new MAC's in their waistbands and rolled out behind Blue.

As they rode to the car lot, they listened to a local radio station called WAMO (106.7):

> *This is going to be the party of the year. Anybody that's somebody will be there. We got the Sinate performing, and everybody know that they the hottest rap group in the city. There will be free champagne to the first five hundred females, and they all get in free before 11:00 P.M. All courtesy of CK Black and the Columbo boys.*

"Ya'll hear that?" Li'l Lock asked.

"Yeah, I heard it, but I guarantee he won't be there," Blue told him.

"They just said he would be there," Li'l Loc replied excited about catching the nigga who killed his pops.

"The nigga don't ever go to the clubs. He just sends his goons in his name," Blue said trying to get Li'l Loc to forget about the party.

"Well, he going to be a few goons short tonight."

"I'm with you on that, cuz," Arab said ready to ride no matter what the cause.

Blue shook his head in agreement, but in the back of his mind he was hoping that they changed their mind about going to the party to catch CK Black slipping.

When they reached the car lot, they paid the jitney and got out of the car. The Jewish guy who owned the lot saw them and walked over to greet Blue, who was an old customer.

"Hey, what's up?" the man asked shaking his hand.

"Paul, these are my young niggas and we looking to spend some money with you."

"Go ahead and look around. If ya'll see something ya'll like, we will discuss business," he told them before walking off.

They looked around the lot and saw all types of fly cars, but once they spotted the two twin GS 300 Lexus black-on-black, they were in love. The price tags on the cars read thirty-eight thousand dollars, which was in their price range.

Blue went to get Paul and they talked the price of the cars down to thirty-five thousand each. After putting together the fictitious paper work, they pulled off the lot in their new whips. Blue was driving the car in front and Arab was in back with Li'l Loc riding shotgun. They headed straight for the rim shop and got the mirrors tinted and chrome dubs on the feet.

Their cars were immaculate and they drove through every hood in the city showing them off. When they got tired of stunting, they headed back to Homewood so they could put together a plan for CK Black's party. After they got back they chilled and plotted for a short while before Blue got up to leave.

"Where you going, cuz," Li'l Loc asked wanting to discuss their plans a little further.

"I got to go make a few runs."

"When you coming back?" Arab asked him.

"I'll be back in time for the party," he replied leaving the house.

After Blue left, Arab spoke up. "He acting real funny," he said voicing his concerns about Blue's action.

"I thought I was the only one to notice it," Li'l Loc said agreeing with him.

"We probably just tripping. I mean we did spank his so-called homie," Arab said.

"Yeah, you right. I tell you one thing, though. If he keep acting like this, we going to have to stop fucking with him."

"Either that or we going to have to kill him," Arab said thinking of the way Blue looked at him when he was filling up the bag with Grim's money.

They were silent for a while, thinking about the situation with Blue, but Li'l Loc shook it off and spoke up, breaking the trance that Arab was in. "Let's go get something to eat," he said standing up.

"From where?" Arab asked.

"Simi's, nigga. You should already know. . . .and I'm driving this time," Li'l Loc said holding his hand out for the keys.

"You don't even know how to drive."

"This is a good time to learn. Anyway, the store is right around the corner."

"You right," Arab said handing the keys over.

They went outside and hopped into the Lex, feeling like they were on top of the world. Li'l Loc started the car and Arab instructed him how to drive as they headed to the store. It seemed as if he were a natural because they made it there without incident, not a scratch or dent.

When they pulled up to the store, all eyes were on them.

"You see how they staring at us?" Li'l Loc said throwing the car in park.

"Yeah, I see 'em," Arab said getting out of the car.

Li'l Loc got out as well, leaving the doors open so every-body could hear the sounds.

"Whose car ya'll got?" one of the onlookers asked as they walked through the crowd.

They looked at each other and shook their heads, ignoring the question as they arrogantly walked into the restaurant. It was their time and the sun was shining on them. From the looks of things, there would be no rain in their future.

"How may I help you?" the cashier asked as they approached the counter.

"Let me get six wings and a Pepsi," Arab replied pulling his money out.

"Give me the same thing," Li'l Loc said reaching in his pocket for his dough.

"Your orders will be done in about ten minutes," the cashier said ringing their orders up.

After paying for their food, they went back outside to see what was cracking in their hood.

Outside they were greeted by Raw who was admiring their car. "What's up, li'l cuz?" he said giving them the Crip handshake.

"What's cracking?" they both replied.

"Ya'll hear about the nigga Wicked getting spanked?" he asked even though he already heard the rumor floating around about them being the ones who killed him.

"When that happen?" Arab asked as if he knew noting about it.

"It happened a couple days ago. It was on the news and everything," Raw told them.

"Niggas got to be more careful," Li'l Loc said getting in the car to turn the music up as loud as it would go.

"Ya'll niggas ridin' real fly. Where ya'll cop this from?" Raw asked about the Lexus.

"A little spot on Route 51," Arab said waving the car off as if it wasn't anything.

"The nigga Blue got one just like it," Li'l Loc told him.

"Ya'll be doing ya'll thing, but ya'll need to watch who ya'll fuck with because this is a cold game."

"What you mean 'watch who we be fuckin' with'?" Li'l Loc asked.

"Never mind, cuz. I was just saying, you know."

"What you saying?" Li'l Loc asked getting out of the car.

"This is between us, right?" Raw asked trying to protect his ass.

"Just say what you was going to say," Arab said getting irritated.

The look on Arab's face had Raw shook, and he knew that if he didn't come out with it, he would have problems. And he definitely didn't want any problems with these two crazy young niggas. "It's about your pops," Raw said getting Li'l Loc's attention.

"What about him?"

"Well, when your pops got killed, word on the streets was Blue had something to do with it. In fact, they say Blue made that call on him."

Even though Blue had been acting strange since the shit with Grim, Li'l Loc still had love for him and he knew that Raw was wrong about him having something to do with the death of his and Brandon's pops.

"That's bullshit . . . and if it was true, then why Blue get shot, too?" Li'l Loc asked taking up for his big homie.

"Who told you that Blue got shot?" Raw asked twisting his face up.

"Blue told me he got shot. He said that when my pops walked to the car, he stayed back a little which is why he didn't get hit up like they did."

"He ever show you the bullet wounds?"

"Nah, but why would he lie?" Li'l Loc asked.

"That's what I'm trying to say, cuz. The reason why he can't show you his bullet wounds is because he don't got none. Right before them niggas came shooting, Blue went into your dad's house. He didn't come back out until the shooting stopped."

"You talking some bullshit," Arab said interrupting their conversation. He knew that Blue was a snake, but he didn't think that he would get his old heads murdered for nothing.

"Like I said, that was the word on the streets back then. I use to look up to your pops and he always showed me love, which is the only reason I'm saying anything. Ya'll can take it how ya'll want," he said stepping off.

After he left, Li'l Loc spoke up. "You hear this nigga?" he asked Arab.

"That nigga just hating. He see us shining and now he want to see us turn on each other."

"You right," Li'l Loc said as they went back into the restaurant to get their food.

After picking up their orders, they hopped in the Lex and headed back to Li'l Loc's spot.

Li'l Loc's head was spinning from everything Raw told him and he didn't know what to believe. Ever since Blue told him that he knew who killed his dad, he was wondering why Blue never retaliated if he loved him so much. *Maybe he did have something to do with it*, he thought to himself. As quickly as the thought entered his head, it left. *Blue is a real nigga*, he said to himself as he pulled up in front of his crib.

After throwing the car in park, he shook Raw's words off and looked Arab in the eyes. "You ready for this party," he asked.

"Cuz, I'm always ready," he answered with his hand on the handle of his MAC.

CHAPTER 17

*R*rring, Rrring, Rrring was the sound that woke Bay Boe up from his deep sleep. "I wonder who the fuck is calling me," he said looking at the caller I.D. He didn't recognize the number, but he answered anyway. "Who this?"

"This CK Black. What it be like?"

"Oh, what up, Blood?" Bay Boe said wondering why he was calling him so early in the week. They hadn't had the work that long, so he hoped that he wasn't calling for the money.

"I know you probably ain't recognize the number and that's because I got rid of my old phone."

"Should I be doing the same?" Bay Boe asked not really wanting to get rid of his new cell phone.

"Yeah, your shit probably hot, too, so dump it as soon as possible."

"I'm a-do that ASAP"

"The other reason I'm calling is because I'm throwing a b-day party tomorrow and I want you and your homies to come through."

"Where is the party going to be at?"

"Down the Strip District at Club Empire."

"We definitely going to be there," Bay Boe assured him.

"I'll see you there, and don't forget to get rid of your phone," CK said before hanging up.

After hanging up, Bay Boe got up and went downstairs to tell his homies about the party.

"Damn, nigga, I thought you was sleep," Pretty Boy said seeing him come down the steps.

"I was, but CK Black just called me and said he having a b-day party tomorrow at Club Empire."

"We ain't really got no time for partying," Pretty Boy said not feeling the club thing.

"It's only one night and we getting money, so we need to celebrate our success," Mr. Boo said.

"We have been hustling hard and we deserve to live it up a little," Snype said agreeing with Mr. Boo.

"You know what, ya'll right," Pretty Boy agreed.

"Let's pitch in and rent a hummer limo or something extreme," Bay Boe suggested.

"A hummer limo sounds good to me. I say we close shop tomorrow so we can get the limo and so we can get fresh for the party," Pretty Boy said making it official. "But, for now let's move this work because I got something to do later on."

"What you got to do that's more important than this?" Bay Boe asked him.

"I promised Ki-Ki that I would take her to the movies tonight."

"That is your wifey, so I guess it's important. Anyway, if you don't keep your word, she going to be on your ass," Bay Boe said laughing.

"Whatever, nigga," Pretty Boy replied with a smile on his face. Bay Boe was definitely right about Ki-Ki. She was a firecracker, feisty as all hell and whenever she didn't get her way, he had to hear her mouth. But she was his baby, so he didn't mind.

They kept moving their work and business was good as always. They were moving six to seven birds a week like clock work and it didn't look like things would slow down any time soon. When nine o'clock hit, Pretty Boy got up to leave.

"I'm out of here," he said putting his Glock on his waist.

"You better hurry up before she come looking for you," Snype said joking.

"I can't believe my homie is pussy whipped," Bay Boe said shaking his head.

"Fuck you, nigga, I ain't pussy whipped."

"Yeah, whatever. So how ya'll getting to the movies," Bay Boe asked walking him to the door.

"I already hollered at Mr. Ray and he said he going to drop us off and pick us up."

"We need to just quit bullshitting and buy some whips," Bay Boe said.

"You right about that, but for now Mr. Ray will do," he replied dapping Bay Boe up.

"Be safe, Ike," Bay Boe told him as he left. He knew that you had to be careful fucking with them movie theatres because a nigga would definitely catch you out there slipping.

Pretty Boy walked to Ki-Ki's house, which was only two blocks away. When he got there, he knocked on the door and waited for a response.

"Who is it?" a female answered.

"It's Brandon. Is Quiana there?"

"About time," Ki-Ki said opening the door to let him in.

"What you mean 'about time'?"

"You were suppose to come get me at seven o'clock and it's already nine."

"You said the movie didn't start until 9:30 P.M. and it would be best if we left at nine," Pretty Boy said defending himself.

"I can't believe you didn't remember the time we was suppose to leave," she said smiling.

"I must have heard you wrong and I apologize for being late," he told her hoping that she would accept his apology.

The puppy dog look on his face made Ki-Ki start laughing.

"What's so funny?"

"You're right, baby. I did say nine o'clock. I was just messing with you."

"You need to stop playing," he said sitting on the living room sofa.

"So how we going to get to the movies without a car?" Ki-Ki asked him.

"I got Mr. Ray taking us. Matter of fact, give me the phone so I can give him directions to your house."

"Get it yourself while I go finished getting dressed," she said going up the steps to her room.

After calling Mr. Ray and telling him where to come pick him up, he went upstairs to see what Ki-Ki was doing.

Ki-Ki heard someone coming up the steps, and when she turned around, Pretty Boy was at her door. "What you doing here?" she asked.

"I'm trying to see what's up with you."

"How do you know my mom ain't in the other room or something?"

"Is she?" he asked looking behind him into the hallway.

"No, she ain't here. She's at work," she said laughing at the nervous face he was making.

"If she at work, then why are we going to the movies when we can make a movie of our own," he said walking towards her.

"Stop being nasty," she said turning away from him.

He walked up behind her and began kissing her on the neck to get something started.

"Our ride will be here any minute," she said trying to get him to stop.

He ignored her comment while lifting her mini skirt up and pushing her panties to the side. "You sure you want me to stop?" he asked caressing her clit.

"No, baby," she leaned back and whispered in his ear.

He played with her clit until her pussy juices started to flow, and then he slid his index finger inside of her, nice and slow.

"That feels good, daddy," she said in between moans.

He slid another finger in her pussy and began to finger fuck her even harder, causing her to scream out in pleasure.

"You like this, don't you?" he asked using his other hand to pull his dick out.

"I love it, daddy," she replied pushing her ass back against his dick.

It was then that he removed his fingers and pounded his dick into her soaking wet pussy. "I want you to come on this dick," he said fucking her fast and hard.

She threw her pussy back at him while biting her lips to keep from screaming too loud. The way he was fucking her had her whole body tingling and she knew that it wouldn't be long before she came.

Ki-Ki's pussy was bomb, and he couldn't control himself too much longer. He sped up his pace, gripping her thighs tight as he beat her pussy out the frame, feeling himself close to coming as well.

"Fuck me harder, baby, I'm about to come," she screamed out, throwing her pussy back at him as hard as she could.

The feeling of her coming threw him over the edge and he nutted inside of her as her body shook.

"Damn, you got some bomb," he said trying to regain his composure.

As soon as they were done, they heard Mr. Ray outside beeping the horn.

"See, he here already and I'm not even dressed."

"Just take your time. I'll go downstairs and tell him we will be ready in a minute," Pretty Boy said kissing her before heading down the steps.

After letting Mr. Ray know that they would be a short while, he went back in the house to wait for her. He sat downstairs on the couch, not wanting to be caught in Ki-Ki's room if her mom came home.

Ki-Ki came down the steps fifteen minutes later ready to go.

"Now we really going to be late," Pretty Boy said getting up from the couch.

"Whose fault is that," she replied smiling.

"So you ain't enjoy it?" he asked.

"What you think?"

"Well, it was worth it," he said leading her outside to their ride.

"So which theatre we gong to?" Mr. Ray asked as they got in the car.

"Loews on the Waterfront," Pretty Boy told him.

Mr. Ray knew the location and it didn't take long for them to get there, but their little sexcapade still made them late for their movie.

When they pulled up in front of the theatre, Pretty Boy adjusted the Glock on his waist, paid the jitney and got out of the car.

The movie was jam-packed, which was the norm for a Friday night. He was hoping that he didn't have any problems, but if he did, he was more than ready for them. He saw a couple of people eyeing him and he guessed it was because of his attire. He had on his all-black Dickie suit with a black Pirate's fitted hat and his red flag hanging out of his back right pocket repping hard.

"Damn, it's packed in here," he said to Ki-Ki, not really feeling the attention he was getting.

"It's always like this on Fridays and Saturdays," she said looking around to see if she knew anybody in the crowd.

"So you want to see *State Property*, right?" he asked walking over to the ticket booth.

"If it ain't too far into the movie,"

"Well, won't you get us some snacks while I get the tickets," he said waiting in line.

"I need some money," she said holding her hand out with a smile on her face.

"Don't you always,' he said handing her a hundred dollar bill.

After getting the tickets, he went to the snack concession stand to meet up with Ki-Ki. When he got there, he spotted a nigga trying to talk to her.

"Yo, Blood, that's my girl," he said grabbing her hand.

"So what you saying, cuz?" the guy said looking him up and down.

Before the situation could go any further, Ki-Ki stepped in to diffuse things. "Don't even pay him any attention," she said leading Pretty Boy away from the Crip.

"You got that one, Ike," Pretty Boy said as he and Ki-Ki went to catch what little bit of the movie they didn't miss.

An hour later they came out of the movie theatre completely satisfied.

"That was a good-ass movie," Pretty Boy said as they waited out front for Mr. Ray to come pick them up.

"It was good, wasn't it?" Ki-Ki agreed.

After waiting for five minutes, Pretty Boy decided to go back in the theatre to use the bathroom. "If he come, tell him I will be right back," he told her before going back inside.

As soon as he walked into the bathroom, he knew it was going to be a problem.

"What do we have here?" the Crip he had the argument with earlier asked.

"What up, Blood?" Pretty Boy said reaching for the gun on his waist. Before he could pull it out, one of the Crips punched him from behind, knocking him into the wall.

"Get him, cuz," one of the Crips said as they all began punching and kicking him while he was down.

"Fuck this," Pretty Boy said letting off a shot into the crowd.

The single shot didn't stop any of the Crips from jumping on him. One of them even tried to pry the gun out of his hand.

Not wanting to die, he began to squeeze off round after round. He wasn't even aiming; he was just trying to shoot whoever was in the bathroom.

After letting off a quick twenty rounds, all of the Crips were on the ground bleeding from one place or another. He looked around, and the first thing he thought to himself was, *Fuck, I got to get out of here*. He then pulled his bandana out of his pocket and put it over his face before leaving the bathroom.

He was still a little woozy from the blow to the back of his head and he practically stumbled out of the theatre with the panicking crowd, trying his best to blend in. When he got out front, he saw Mr. Ray's car there waiting for him. *Thank God*, he said to himself, getting in the front seat and tucking the hot burner in his waist at the same time.

"What happened in there?" Ki-Ki asked worried that Pretty Boy was the cause of it.

"Some niggas was fighting and shooting," he said checking the rear view mirror for any signs of police.

"So where we headed to?" Mr. Ray asked wondering what his favorite customer had gotten him into.

"Drop her off at home and take me to Bay Boe's spot."

"Why can't I come with you?" Ki-Ki asked upset.

"Because I got some moves to make," he said not going into detail. He knew that she would get an attitude, but he didn't give a fuck.

"So you just going to do whatever you want?" she asked trying to start an argument.

He didn't even feed into her bullshit. He had bigger things on his mind to worry about—like whether or not he killed one of them niggas in the bathroom.

Back on the Hill, they pulled up in front of Ki-Ki's house and she got out, slamming the door with a serious attitude.

"I'll call you later," he told her trying to calm her down a little bit, but he didn't receive a reply.

Ki-Ki didn't want him to see the tears in her eyes as she walked into the house. She was silently praying that he wasn't involved in the incident at the movies because she didn't want to lose him.

When they pulled up in front of Bay Boe's house, he paid Mr. Ray and got out of the car. Bay Boe must have been watching the monitors because he opened the door before Pretty Boy's foot touched the first step.

"Why you back so soon?" Bay Boe asked him.

"I got into some shit at the movies, so I just dropped Ki-Ki off and came straight here," he replied pulling his Glock out and setting it on the table.

"What happened?" Bay Boe asked him.

Pretty Boy told him the whole story, and when he was done, everybody in the room became silent.

Snype picked up the walkie-talkie and radioed LK and Bundy who were on the corner, posted with their choppers. "Ya'll niggas be on point out there because Pretty Boy had some problems at the movie theatre."

"We always on point," they both replied ready for whatever came their way.

Mr. Boo picked up Pretty Boy's hot Glock from the table. "I'll get rid of this for you," he said before leaving the house.

"Don't even sweat that shit. Anyway, I got some good news for you," Bay Boe told him.

"What type of good news?" Pretty Boy asked, his mind still stuck back in the movie theatre. *I wonder if the cameras could tell if that was me leaving the bathroom* is what he was thinking before Bay Boe interrupted his thoughts with the good news.

"I got this nigga who said he know where we can get any type of whip we want for straight cash," Bay Boe told him.

"So when we going to make it happen?" he asked brightening up a little at the sound of getting a new car.

"First thing in the morning."

"Well, I'm a-go to the crib and get some rest," Pretty Boy said getting up to leave. He had too much shit on his mind to focus on hustling.

"Take my gun just in case you get into some shit on the way home," Snype said handing him his Glock.

He left the spot after dapping all of his homies up and went straight home, going straight to his room once he entered his house.

He laid down in bed fully clothed and tried to go to sleep. But he was tossing and turning all night, wondering if the cameras caught him going in or coming out of the bathroom at the movie theatre. He also wondered if he killed any of the Crips who tried to jump him. These were the thoughts running through his mind for the next two hours before he finally drifted off to sleep.

CHAPTER 18

"Brandon...Brandon...get up, baby!" his Grams screamed while standing over his body.

He had two bullets in his chest and he was bleeding profusely. He could hear the sirens in the background and this was the first time he welcomed the sound. *Damn, this is how I'm gong to die,* he thought to himself.

"Brandon . . . Brandon . . . wake up!" Grams continued to scream. She started shaking him to keep him from drifting off into a never-ending sleep. It was at this time that he woke up from his bad dream in confusion, grabbing his chest and gasping for air.

"Boy, what's wrong with you?" Grams asked before going to get a wet cloth to wipe the sweat from his face. A few seconds later she came back with the cloth and handed it to him so he could get himself together. "We going to have to go to the doctor to get you a check-up," she said giving him a worried look.

"I'm cool, Grams. I just had another bad dream."

"Well, I'm going to make another appointment anyway. Now get up and go see what your friend wants at the door."

"What friend?" he asked getting out of bed.

"Bay Boo or Baby Boe or whatever his name is," she said shaking her head at the names kids had these days.

"You mean Bay Boe," he said laughing as he headed to the door.

When he got downstairs, he opened the door and let him in the house. "What up, Ike?" he asked dapping his homie up.

"The nigga who got the hook-up for the cars is out front, so get dressed and grab some money."

"How much do I need," Pretty Boy asked before going back to his room.

"Just bring twenty thousand," Bay Boe told him.

"I'll be right back," he said going to his room to grab the change and throw on some different clothes.

After putting on a new outfit, he went into his shoe box to pull his money out. He had about a hundred grand in his stash now, so the twenty grand he was about to spend wasn't anything. When he got done counting out the money, he stuffed it into his pant's pocket before putting the shoe box back. He then reached under the mattress and pulled his Glock out, tucking it into his waistband before leaving his room.

He stopped at his grams' room to tell her he was leaving and all she said was to be safe. She knew that he was knee deep in the streets when she found the money stashed under his bed while cleaning his room. She just prayed that he didn't end up dead like his father. Thinking of his father—her son—made her pray for Brandon as he went down the steps and out the door.

He and Bay Boe went outside and hopped in the car connect's 2002 Expedition. The rest of the squad was in the truck as well.

"So where we going?" Bay Boe asked the connect, whose name was Mr. Tone.

"It's a car lot up Ohio about an hour outside of Pittsburgh," he replied before pulling off.

And hour and twenty minutes later they pulled up in the car lot, and the first thing they noticed were the two Denali trucks sitting out front. They all got out and walked over to the two trucks to check them out while Mr. Tone went to get the sales rep.

"These trucks is fly than a muthafucka," Snype said looking through the window at the butter-soft tan leather interior.

"I wonder how much they want for them?" Bay Boe said searching for the price tags.

"It say right here that they want forty-two thousand apiece," Pretty Boy told him.

"Let's just pitch in and get both of them, since we always gong to be riding together anyway," Mr. Boo suggested.

"I see ya'll interested in these trucks," the sales rep said walking up behind them followed by Mr. Tone.

"How much ya'll want for them if we paying straight cash?" Pretty Boy asked.

"Forty-six thousand apiece and that includes my fee," the sales rep told them.

"We'll take them," Bay Boe said pulling his money out of his pocket.

"Let's all go in and get some papers signed with your Uncle Tone," the sales rep said leading them into the dealership.

It took them an hour to get all the paper work handled. The trucks cost them ninety-two thousand in cash, and they paid Mr. Tone eight stacks to sign as a co-signer to the fictitious names they were registering the cars under.

When they were done with everything, they hopped in the trucks and drove off. Pretty Boy was driving the all-red Denali and Bay Boe was driving the pearly-white one. They were three deep in each truck, all of them smiling from ear to ear as they rode back to the city.

When they got to Pittsburgh, they headed straight for the rim shop. After paying fifteen thousand to get twenty-six inch spinners on both of the trucks, they headed downtown to go clothes shopping so they could be fresh for CK Black's party.

CHAPTER 19

"That's a long-ass line," Li'l Loc said hopping out of the passenger seat of his and Arab's GS-300 Lexus. The line was so long it stretched around the block.

Blue hopped out of his brand-new Lexus and walked over to Li'l Loc and Arab. "Damn, you see all these hoes out here?" he said trying to take their minds off of CK Black.

"Fuck these hoes, nigga. I'm just trying to get the nigga who killed my dad and that's it," Li'l Loc said wondering how Blue could even think of a bitch when they were trying to avenge his pop's death.

"Whatever, cuz. Let's just get in this club," Blue said heading straight to the front of the line.

They each gave the bouncer a hundred dollars and went in without being searched or asked for their I.D.s. Once inside, they began to look around in search of the reason they were there, which was to kill CK Black or anybody affiliated with him.

There was wall-to-wall people in the club, and you could barely move through the crowd without bumping someone. They went straight to the back of the club and posted with their backs against the wall, with murder on their minds and no mercy in their hearts.

"What's up? Ya'll niggas want something to drink?" Blue asked them looking around for a bitch to holler at.

"Hell, nah, cuz . . . you trippin?" Li'l Loc replied.

"We ain't got no time to be getting drunk. We here to handle some business," Arab added looking at Blue as if he had lost his mind.

"Well, nigga, I'm going to go get some bottles. Ya'll can stand here and look all stiff and shit by ya'll damn selves," Blue said before heading to the bar.

When he was gone, Li'l Loc and Arab looked at each other and shook their heads, wondering what the fuck Blue's problem was. He was acting real funny and they were both starting to think about the things Raw told them earlier that day about Blue having something to do with his pop's death.

*   *   *   *   *

Meanwhile, Pretty Boy and his homies were in the VIP area with CK Black and his squad drinking Rose and living the good life.

"Ya'll enjoying ya'll selves?" CK asked dapping all of them up. He had love for his young Hill niggas and he planned to make a lot more money with them in the future, as long as they stayed loyal.

"Hell, yeah, we enjoying ourselves," Bay Boe said sipping his champagne.

"What about you, Pretty Boy? You having a good time?"

"Yeah, this party is dope," Pretty Boy replied putting his glass in the air as if he was toasting him.

"I'm glad to hear ya'll both enjoying ya'll selves. Here go a little something to make it a little more interesting," he said handing them an ounce of purple haze and a few boxes of dutchees.

Bay boe took the weed and dapped CK up. "Good looking, Ike," he said before taking one of the dutchees out to roll up.

"If ya'll need anything else, just let me know," CK said dapping the rest of them up before walking away.

*   *   *   *   *

They had been posted in the back of the club for at least a half hour and there was no sign of CK Black or anybody in his circle. Tired of waiting, Li'l Loc tapped Arab on the shoulder. "Let's get the fuck out of here," he said frustrated.

"What about CK Black?"

"Blue was right. That nigga ain't going to show up."

"Let's go look for Blue first," Arab said heading into the crowd with Li'l Loc by his side.

Since they didn't know what CK Black looked like, Blue was supposed to be their eyes in the club. They figured that since he hadn't come to them saying that he spotted CK, then he must not have been in the club. But, in reality, even if Blue would have seen CK, he wouldn't have given them the heads up.

As they searched around the dance floor for Blue, the DJ began making an announcement, turning everybody's attention to the stage: "I want ya'll to give it up for the man of the hour, my homie, the notorious CK Black!"

CK Black walked up on the stage followed by a few of his homies and grabbed the mike. "Yo, ya'll know who I be. This is ya boy, CK Black, and once again I'm doing it big for my b-day. For the next hour, bottles of Moet is on me, so enjoy yourselves," he said before leaving the stage.

That nigga Blue is a snake, Li'l Loc thought to himself.

"Lying-ass nigga," Arab said looking Li'l Loc in the eyes, thinking the same thing.

"Fuck that. I'm a-kill this nigga right now," Li'l Loc said pulling his gun out, heading towards CK Black, who was walking across the dance floor surrounded by his goons.

"You can't do it right here," Arab said grabbing him by the shoulder.

"Why not?" Li'l Loc said with tears of frustration in his eyes.

"Look around you, nigga," Arab told him pointing at all the potential witnesses.

"So what we going to do?" Li'l Loc asked tucking the gun back in his waist and wiping the tears from his eyes.

"First we going to look for Blue, then we going to go wait for the nigga in the parking lot."

"Come on then," Li'l Loc said walking through the crowd in search of Blue.

When they found him, he was on the dance floor grooving with a broad as if he didn't just see CK Black on the stage making an announcement.

"Damn, cuz, I though you said CK Black don't ever come to his b-day parties?" Li'l Loc asked with anger in his voice.

The broad that Blue was dancing with heard Li'l Loc's comment and spoke up, "He never misses his parties."

This confirmed their suspicions about Blue, and they knew that after they dealt with CK Black, they would have to deal with him.

"Come on, Blue, let's go outside and wait for him," Li'l Loc whispered low enough so the girl couldn't hear him.

"Just let that shit go, cuz," Blue said waving him off.

"What the fuck you mean, let it go? That nigga killed my dad," Li'l Loc replied, tears running down his cheek. He was angry that the nigga who killed his pops was in the club with him and he wasn't dead yet. He was also hurt by the way Blue was betraying him. He looked up to Blue, and he was the closest thing he had to a father since his pops was murdered.

"Look, cuz, we can handle that shit some other time. Just not right now."

"Fuck that nigga, cuz," Arab said loud enough for Blue to hear as he grabbed Li'l Loc's arm and walked him to the door. Once outside they went to their car and waited patiently for the party to end.

After they left, Blue went up to the VIP area to say happy b-day to his cousin, CK Black.

Back when B-braze first introduced him and his old heads to CK, Blue noticed that it was his aunt's son, but neither he nor CK said anything about it. In fact it was then that CK Black realized that they were not from East Hills, but he still served them because of Blue, who was his first cousin. He figured that the Crips were just lying about where they were from so they could score some work. The last thing he thought was they were trying to rob him.

At first Blue tried to convince his old heads to forget about the robbery, especially since CK Black was serving them birds for the low low. But they already had their minds set, and they weren't trying to hear anything he was saying, so he just went along with it.

He decided to use it as an opportunity to get Li'l Loc's dad out of the way, so he could have Li'l Loc's mom all to himself. Or at least, that's how he thought it would happen.

After the robbery he got in touch with CK Black and let him know what went down. CK Black let him off the hook, being as though they were family, but not without a price to pay. He told Blue that he would have to return as much of the money as possible, and he would also have to set up his old heads. In return, not only would CK Black let him live, he would give him fifty thousand dollars.

Blue did just that. He robbed the stash houses and then called the police to let them grab their guns and the little work left behind. He then returned all the money and work they had to CK Black and put in a call on his old heads, which got them sprayed in a drive-by.

In his mind it was all worth it, because he now had Keisah—Li'l Loc's mom—and she was all he really wanted. He justified his actions by looking out for CJ and Brandon over the years. They didn't know, but he kept them safe in the hood. He figured that if he kept them out of the streets, he would also keep them away from the truth about their fathers' deaths.

By turning Li'l Loc on to the game and telling him who killed his father, he was going against everything he believed would keep the truth from coming out, and now he was paying for it.

CK Black saw him entering the VIP area and he walked over to greet him.

"What the fuck you doing here, Blue?" he asked dapping his cousin up. Even though Blue set up his homies for him, he still looked at Blue as a snake and he wouldn't touch him with a ten-foot pole.

"Happy b-day," Blue said sensing the same tension he always felt when greeting his cousin. He knew CK Black didn't fully trust him and he didn't blame him. Blue was a cold-blooded snake and, truth was, if he ever got a chance to rob CK again, he would take him for everything he had.

"Thanks," CK replied.

"I need to talk to you about some serious shit, cuz," Blue said pulling him to the side.

"What you talking about?" CK asked wondering what scam Blue was trying to run.

"I know you remember that shit that happened with my old heads back in the day."

"How the fuck could I forget?"

"Well, one of them niggas' sons is out front in an all-black GS 300 Lexus. He and his homie waiting for you to come out so they can kill you."

"How you know this?" CK asked wondering what part Blue was playing in the set up.

"I'm just giving you a heads up. How I know about it is irrelevant. Whether you want to take heed or not is up to you, but I suggest you watch yourself."

"Thanks for the info, but I'm always on point, so I ain't sweating them niggas," CK said before taking a sip of his bottled water.

All the while they were talking, Pretty Boy was watching them.

"You know that nigga?" Bay Boe asked about Blue.

"Yeah, I know him. He was my pop's young nigga, and he mess around with my brother's mom."

Right after Blue left, CK called over one of his goons, and after whispering something in his ear, he rushed out of the VIP area.

Pretty Boy watched the scene play out before turning back to his Rose. In his mind, he wondered why CK was conversing with a known Crip.

*   *   *   *   *

While Li'l Loc and Arab were sitting in the car smoking a dutchee, a nigga walked up and tapped on the passenger side window.

"Who the fuck is this?" Arab said to Li'l Loc, pointing his gun at the door as he rolled the window down.

"Yo, Blood, you got a light?" CK Black's goon asked, cigarette hanging from his mouth.

Arab sensed that something was wrong, and before the Blood could raise his gun, he began shooting through the door.

Li'l Loc heard the shots and he hit the gas, skirting out of the parking lot, almost hitting a few cars on the way.

"Why you shoot that nigga? We was supposed to be waiting for CK Black," Li'l Loc said slowing down to the speed limit so they wouldn't get pulled over.

"He was one of CK Black's goons," Arab said setting the smoking gun on his lap.

"How the fuck you know? Just 'cause he was a Blood don't mean he was one of CK Black's goons."

"I'm telling you, cuz, I seen that nigga on the stage with CK Black when he made that announcement."

"I wonder how the fuck he know what car we was in," Li'l Loc wondered out loud.

"It had to be Blue's snake ass," Arab said tightening his grip on the gun.

"Hell, yeah," Li'l Loc agreed.

Everything that Raw told them was making sense, and they couldn't wait to catch up with Blue so they could find out why he tried to get them hit.

*   *   *   *   *

Pretty Boy and his homies were in the club having it their way. They were drinking Roses, smoking haze, taking flicks and stuntin' hard.

Not too long after Blue left, they all headed to the dance floor to holler at the hoes, and to show off the jewelery they were wearing and the matching all-red minks that they were all stuntin' in. When they were on their way back to the VIP area, Bay Boe accidentally bumped into a Crip nigga, causing the Crip to spill his drink.

"Watch where the fuck you going," the Crip said pushing him.

"First of all, Blood, I ain't your cuz, so watch who the fuck you talking to like that," Bay Boe replied.

"Nigga, do you know who the fuck I am?" the Crip asked lifting his shirt up to show the butt of his gun.

"I don't give a fuck who you is," Bay Boe said opening his mink up to show the hundred-round Calico hanging from his neck by a shoe string. It was then that the rest of Bay Boe's homies noticed what was going on and stepped up to back their homie.

"What the fuck is up, Blood?" Pretty Boy asked, pulling his Glock out and cocking it back, ready to start shooting in the club.

"Ain't no problems. I was just leaving," the Crip said walking back over to where his homies were standing.

Pretty Boy and his homies went back to VIP to finish partying. They were all high and drunk, feeling like they were untouchable, and they partied until last call.

When it was time to roll, they said their last happy b-days and then headed to their waiting Denalis with a few broads following behind them, wanting to get smutted. Once outside, they hopped into their trucks and sped off, not paying any attention to their surroundings. If they were on point, they would have noticed the Crip niggas they had the altercation with following behind them.

Pretty Boy didn't have any plans of smutting the females out with his homies, so he had Bay Boe follow him to his grams house, where he was going to give the car to LK before hooking up with Ki-Ki. When they pulled up in front of Pretty Boy's house, the Crips rode past them in a blue Maxima and circled the block. They parked on a side street and hopped out of the car. Two of them had choppers and the other had a hand gun.

Before Pretty Boy went in the house, Bay Boe hopped out of the truck to dap him up and let him know that he would see him in the A.M. As the Crips rounded the corner, he was the first to spot them. He didn't say a word because he was too busy reaching for the Calico under his mink. As soon as he reached the trigger, he let off a burst of rounds. *Pop-pop-pop-pop-pop-pop* was the noise the Calico made as bullets tore into one of the Crips.

The Crips immediately began to return fire, striking Pretty Boy in the stomach and shoulder, causing him to fall to the ground in pain.

The rest of their homies hopped out of the trucks and began to spray rounds, backing the Crips down.

The Crips were getting low on rounds, so they retreated back to their car, dragging the Crip who was injured by Bay Boe's Calico. After hopping into their car, they skirted off with LK right behind them letting off a burst of rounds with his MAC that shattered the back window of the Maxima.

Pretty Boy's grams came running out of the house after the gunfire ceased. She began to panic at the sight of her grandson laying on the sidewalk bleeding.

"Get up, Brandon, get up!" she screamed trying to lift him up from the concrete.

It was just like the dream he'd been having. He even recognized the sounds of the sirens in the background. *So this is how I'm going to die*, he thought to himself before blacking out.

CHAPTER 20

The next day, after receiving surgery, Pretty Boy came to in the hospital. When he awoke, he saw all of his homies standing around the hospital bed.

"What up, Blood?" Bay Boe asked seeing his eyes open.

"I'm good," he replied feeling groggy with a serious case of cotton mouth. "Could somebody grab me some water?" he added in a low whisper.

"I got you, Ike," Snype said leaving the room.

"I thought you wasn't going to make it," Grams said crying.

"Don't cry, Grams, I'll be aiight" he said trying to console her. He knew if she continued to cry, then the tears would flow from his own eyes and he didn't want to cry in front of his homies.

Before the tears could flow, Snype came back in the room with a glass of water. "Here you go, homie," he said helping Pretty Boy take a sip from the cup.

"I'm a-go call CJ and let him know what happened. Maybe he can get a ride over here to see you," Grams said before leaving the room.

While he had been on the Hill getting money, he had not thought about what his brother was doing. He felt guilty, thinking that maybe CJ needed his help and he wasn't there to extend his hand, even though he was in a position to do so. *Fuck it*, he thought to himself, knowing that he couldn't change the past, but he could do better in the future.

After making a promise to himself to stay in touch with his brother no matter what, he shook him from his mind and focused on the situation at hand. "Ya'll find out who them niggas was?" he whispered breaking the silence.

"It was the Crip niggas that I got into it with at the club, but you don't have to worry about nothing because we going to get them niggas," Bay Boe told him. He felt like he was the reason Pretty Boy got shot, because he had started the argument with the Crips in the club.

"That goes without saying . . . retaliation is a must," Pretty Boy said knowing that his homies would ride for him at the drop of a dime.

"Now that we know you're aiight, we going to go handle them niggas," Bay Boe said before he and the rest of their homies filed out of the room with murder on their minds and in their hearts.

As soon as they were gone, Pretty Boy dozed off, hoping that they caught the niggas who shot him and showed them no mercy.

* * * * *

CJ and Arab sat in the house waiting for Blue to come home so they could confront him. Blue had been out all night and his absence further confirmed their suspicions about him.

"CJ, come here!" his mom hollered from her room.

She probably want to know why Blue didn't come home, he thought to himself before going to see what she wanted. "What up?" he asked walking into her room.

"Brandon's grandma just called and said he got shot. She want to know if you can make it to the hospital."

After finding out which hospital his brother was at, he ran downstairs and grabbed his MAC from under the couch.

"What's wrong, cuz?" Arab asked seeing the look on his homie's face.

"Brandon got hit up," Li'l Loc said rushing out the door.

Arab grabbed his gun and followed behind, wondering what happened to his friend.

On the way to the hospital, Li'l Loc couldn't help but feel responsible for Brandon getting shot. He knew that he was in a position to help his brother and he hadn't even reached out. Although he couldn't change the past, he planned to do things better in the future.

When they arrived at the hospital, they parked their car and went in the hospital to Pretty Boy's room. The first person they saw when they entered the room was Grams, who was standing over the hospital bed looking down on her grandson.

"What's up, Grams?" Li'l Loc said walking up behind her.

She turned around in surprise, happy to see her other baby. "How you doing, CJ?" she asked giving him a long hung.

"I'm fine, but how is he doing," he said pointing at Pretty Boy who appeared to be asleep.

"I'm good," Pretty Boy said waking up at the sound of his brother's voice.

"Damn, cuz, what happened?" Li'l Loc asked looking at his brother laying in the hospital bed. You could hear the emotion in his voice and the tears began to stream down his face.

Arab couldn't even speak because of the anger he was feeling at the sight of his homie hit up. He just sat back and watched as Li'l Loc broke down, knowing that if they ever caught the person responsible, they would have hell to pay.

"I'm going to leave ya'll alone," Grams said hugging Li'l Loc and Arab one more time before leaving the room.

"It's been a long time," Pretty Boy said smiling once his grams was out of the room.

"I know, we been busy robbing these bitch-ass niggas out here," Arab said showing him the iced-out chain around his neck.

"I wish you was with us, because we them niggas in the hood now," Li'l Loc told him.

"I been doing aiiright for myself as well," Pretty Boy told them.

"So what you been doing that got you hit up?" Li'l Loc asked.

"Niggas just jealous cause me and my squad getting money moving birds and what not."

"So who was it?" Arab asked ready to retaliate.

"Some Crips that me and my homies got into it with down Club Empire last night. We was down there for the nigga CK Black's b-day party."

"Hold on . . . what CK Black you talking about?" Li'l Loc asked not believing what he was hearing.

"CK Black from Garfield. Me and my niggas be scoring major work off of him."

"We was at that party, too, and one of CK Black's goons tried to run down on us," Arab told him.

"What he try to get at ya'll for?" Pretty Boy asked them confused.

"I don't know how to tell you this, but CK Black got both of our dads killed. The reason why we was at the club was to kill him, but the nigga Blue snaked us and tried to get us hit," Li'l Loc said leaving out the part about the shooting in the parking lot.

"Who told you CK Black got our dad's killed?" Pretty Boy asked hoping there was some type of flaw in the story. He didn't want to believe that he was fucking with the nigga who was responsible for killing his pops.

"Blue told me the whole story about how our fathers robbed CK Black, which led to their getting killed in a drive-by. The nigga Raw also confirmed it," Li'l Loc told him.

"I did see the nigga Blue at the club last night. He came into the VIP section and said something to CK Black before leaving out. As soon as he was gone, CK Black called over one of his goons and whispered something in his ear that caused him to shoot out of the room as if he had something important to go handle."

"What was CK Black's goon wearing?" Arab asked wanting to know if it was the same person he hit up, although he already had a feeling that it was.

"He had on a black and red Negro League coat with a matching fitted hat."

"I knew that nigga Blue snaked us," Arab said after Pretty Boy described the nigga he shot to a tee.

"I wonder why he tried to get us hit?" Li'l Loc said trying to figure out what Blue was getting out of it.

"It don't even matter. We just need to find him and deal with him accordingly. But first we going to handle the niggas who shot you," Arab said ready to ride.

"Don't worry about the niggas who shot me, because my homies out there riding on them. Just go handle Blue and I'll put together a plan to get the nigga CK Black."

"Aiight, nigga, keep your head up," Li'l Loc and Arab both said before leaving to go handle their business.

After leaving the hospital, they hopped in their Lexus and went back to Li'l Loc's house to see if Blue had showed up since they were gone.

When they pulled up, they noticed Blue's car parked out front and they went into the house to greet him.

Blue was sitting on the couch as if he didn't know what had happened to them last night.

"Damn, Blue, where was you at?" Li'l Loc asked pulling his MAC out and setting it on his lap.

"I told ya'll niggas to leave that shit alone," Blue said smoking his dutch.

"Fuck all that. We ain't sweating that nigga CK Black," Arab said changing the subject.

"Good, because that nigga is untouchable, and any time somebody go up against him, they end up on the losing side."

"That's why we going to leave him alone, but we do have this lick that you might be interested in," Arab told him.

Li'l Loc didn't know what he was talking about, but he went along with him knowing that he must have a plan.

"What lick you talking about?" Blue asked always down to hit a nice robbery.

"From what me and Loc heard, when Wicked got killed, he left behind a hundred thousand at his mom's house," Arab said smiling at how easy it was to bait Blue.

"Is the person you got the info off official?" Blue asked.

"Hell, yeah. We bumped into his baby mom when we left the club last night, and after we smutted her out she told us everything. All she want is a small cut so she can buy a new car," Li'l Loc said chiming in.

"So where do his moms stay?" Blue asked.

"Right on Orphan Street. I know the exact house and everything," Arab told him.

"Well, let's go get it," Blue said eager to put some more money in his pocket. He knew that if their information was correct, then there would probably be way more money in the house because Wicked was paid for real.

"We going to take our car," Li'l Loc said getting up from the couch.

They all headed outside and jumped into Arab and Lil Loc's Lexus with Arab at the wheel. On their way to Larimer, they were all bobbing their heads to a song from DMX's old album, called "Use to be my dog."

Blue was bobbing his head to the music as well as they pulled up on Orphan Street and parked. Blue didn't know that the words coming from the stereo were meant for him, so he was oblivious to what was about to happen.

Li'l Loc got out of the car with Blue following them.

"We got to go through the side," Arab said letting Blue get in front of them. Before they could reach the back of the house, he raised his gun and shot Blue in the back, causing him to fall to the ground, dropping his gun in the process.

"I'm hit, cuz," Blue said not knowing where the shot had come from.

"Turn your bitch-ass over," Li'l Loc said kicking him in the side.

"You shot me, cuz," Blue said realizing that he had been crossed.

"Nigga, you tried to get us killed and you set my dad up," Li'l Loc said picking Blue's gun up before he could get to it.

"Whoever told you that is a fucking liar," Blue said with pain in his voice as he tried to plea for his life.

"Brandon told us that he seen you talking to CK Black in the club, and now it's time to pay for your actions," Li'l Loc said cocking his gun back.

"Hold on, cuz. CK Black is my family and that's why I was talking to him, but I swear I ain't set your dad up."

"That explains everything," Li'l Loc said pulling the trigger, leaving brains and blood all over the concrete.

Just to make sure that he was dead, Arab let off a burst of rounds into Blue's lifeless body.

They then ran to their car and hopped in, leaving Blue slumped on the side of the house.

CHAPTER 21

"When they gong to let me leave?" Pretty Boy asked
Grams. He had been in the hospital for a week and

his wounds had healed nicely. The bullets hadn't hit any main arteries, so for the most part he was good.

Right after Li'l Loc and Arab left the hospital, Ki-Ki showed up and stayed by his side for most of the week, coming to check up on him every day. He hadn't seen Bay Boe and his homies or Li'l Loc and Arab since his first day in the hospital, but he followed what they were doing every day on the news. He knew that Blue was dead and the Crips who hit him were catching hell.

"You should be able to leave today at two o'clock," Grams told him.

He looked at the clock on the wall and saw that it was only twelve o'clock.

"I'm a-go see what's taking so long for your lunch to come," Grams said before leaving the room.

After she left, he turned the television on and clicked to the news. The first thing he saw was his face. He turned the volume up and listened closely: *This man is wanted for the murder of Mark Johnson and the shooting of several others at Loew's Theatre last Friday. If you have any information on his whereabouts, please contact us at 412-555-0212.*

"I can't believe this shit," he said turning the TV off and getting out of bed to get dressed. What he had just seen had him shook, and he knew that he had to get out of there in a hurry before the doctors caught on.

While he was getting dressed, Grams came walking back into the room. "Where you think you going?" she asked, food in hand.

"The doctor came by and said it was cool if I left early."

"Let's get out of here then," she said setting the food down and helping him with his bags.

They made it out of the hospital without any problems and, after dropping his bags off at home, he headed to Bay Boe's house to see what was poppin'. Before he could knock on the door, Bay Boe opened it up. "Hurry up," he said ushering him in the house.

"What's wrong?" Pretty Boy asked wondering if they saw his face on the news as well.

"You ain't see the news?" Bay Boe asked confirming what Pretty Boy already knew.

"Nigga, your face been all over it, and I think they looking for us because of all them murders on the North Side," Snype said just as shook as Pretty Boy was.

"The hood been hot as hell. That's why we have not been back to the hospital to check up on you," Mr. Boo told him.

"And the spot been slow because they arresting everybody out there," Bay Boe said shaking his head at what had been going on.

"Shop been closed for the past few days and we going to have to pay CK Black soon," Bundy said worried that they were not going to be able to make the money to pay CK back with the way things were going.

"We ain't got to pay that nigga shit . . . fuck CK Black!" Pretty Boy said with anger in his voice.

"What you mean, fuck CK Black?" LK asked not understanding why he was mad at their connect.

"That nigga got my dad killed, and he tried to get my brother killed the night of his party."

"Who told you that?" Bay Boe asked.

"My brother CJ and my homie Arab came to the hospital right after ya'll left and they told me everything I'm telling ya'll."

"Do you trust their info?" Bay Boe asked. In his eyes, CK Black was the realest nigga ever and he hated to hear that he tried to harm his homie's family.

"I trust their info one hundred per cent," Pretty Boy replied.

"Well, what do you want to do about it?" Bay Boe asked.

"I'm trying to kill that nigga and rob him," Pretty Boy replied wanting to avenge his dad's death.

"You know them niggas be out there on point with they walkie-talkies, and he got the cameras outside his spot," Bay Boe said.

"It's cool. I got the perfect plan, but my brother and my homie Arab coming with us."

"We going to ride with you no matter what, Blood," Bay Boe told him and everybody else nodded their heads in agreement.

*   *   *   *   *

Li'l Loc and Arab had been ducked off for the past week, trying to figure out their next move. They both felt a little remorse for killing Blue, but they knew it had to be done. They were on their twentieth dutchee of the day, when Li'l Loc decided to turn on the six o'clock news. The first thing he saw was Brandon's face.

"That's Brandon, cuz! Turn the volume up!" Arab said excitedly.

After watching the news report, they turned the TV off before his moms could see and tell Grams.

"You think he did that shit?" Arab asked concerned.

"From the looks of the camera footage they showed, he was definitely stumbling out of the bathroom with his gun in his hand, and they said the other victims is telling."

"Yeah, it look bad, cuz," Arab replied.

After seeing the news, Li'l Loc picked up the phone and called the number that Grams had given him to make sure that his bro was alright.

"Praise the Lord," she said answering after the third ring.

"This is CJ, Grams," he told her.

"How you doing, baby?"

"I'm fine, Grams, but is Brandon okay?"

"He's fine now. The doctor let him go from the hospital early and he went over his friend's house around he corner."

"You got the address for me?" he asked.

"I sure do. It's twelve Roberts Street. Make sure you stop by here so I can make you something to eat."

"Aiight, Grams, I'll stop by," he assured her before ending the call.

"Is he aiight?" Arab asked after he hung up the phone.

"She said the doctor let him leave the hospital early, so he good. We got to swing through the Hill District to meet up with him," Li'l Loc said getting up from the couch.

"What we going to do with these hot-ass guns?" Arab asked knowing that they couldn't keep them after killing Blue with them.

"We might need to hold on to them, being as though these is the only guns we got."

"I feel you, but if we going to hook up with Brandon, then we going to be just as hot as he is and, believe me, you don't want to get knocked with that strap," Arab told him.

Li'l Loc thought for a second. He definitely didn't want to get caught with his gun and catch a humbug murder, so he agreed with Arab. "You right, cuz, we need to get rid of these guns ASAP"

"So right after we dump them, then we going to head to the Hill," Arab told him.

Before they could leave the house, Li'l Loc's mom came stumbling into the living room with an empty bottle of E & J. She had been getting drunk all week after finding out that Blue was dead. "Where the fuck do ya'll think ya'll going?" she asked with venom in her voice.

"Go back to your room, Mom," Li'l Loc told her. Even though he didn't get along with his mom, he hated to see her down and depressed.

"Don't tell me what to you, you little murdering piece of shit."

Her words stung Li'l Loc, and he wondered what she was trying to say and why she was trying to hurt his feelings. "What you getting at, Mom?" he asked her.

"You heard what I said. What you think that I don't know about you and your little punk friend killing Blue," she said pointing her accusing finger in Li'l Loc's face.

Arab just stood silent. He was watching how the scene played out. He knew that if she had solid proof that they had killed Blue, then she would have to go as well.

"Where you getting all this bullshit from?" Li'l Loc asked her.

"Ya'll were the last two people to see him alive, and I know that you think he killed your father . . . you hold him responsible. But he wasn't even there. He was here making a phone call," she said with tears in her eyes. They were more for Li'l Loc's dad than Blue.

"Who told you that Blue had something to do with my dad's death?" he asked even though the words she just said let him know that Blue definitely made the call on his pops. It also let him know that his mom knew that Blue made the call as well.

"I know what you're thinking, and Blue could have been talking to anybody on that phone," his mom said trying to plead her case. In fact, she knew who Blue had been talking to because she had been listening from the hallway. It ate her up every day that she might have been able to stop it from happening and didn't.

It was like Li'l Loc was reading her mind. "So you knew that he had something to do with my dad's death, and you was still fucking with him." The tears were streaming down his face . . . he couldn't believe what he was hearing.

"What was I suppose to do? He took care of me and he loved me," she said trying to justify her actions.

"You disgust me," he replied almost in a whisper. He had murder in his eyes and he was one second away from blowing her brains out, but Arab intervened.

"Come on, cuz," Arab said pulling him away. He saw the hate in his friend's eyes and he knew what was coming next.

Before he could leave, his mom ran towards him and tried to stop him from leaving. "I'm sorry, CJ, please forgive me."

"Get the hell off of me," he said pushing her to the floor. He wanted to spit in her face, but he didn't. All he said before stepping out the door was, "I'll be back to pick up my stuff later."

She could tell by the coldness in her son's voice that he would never forgive her. She laid on the floor in a fetal position and cried like a baby. Her son was gone.

They both hopped in their Lex. Arab was at the wheel and Li'l Loc was in the passenger seat, silent as they sped away. After driving a few blocks, they pulled over to a sewer. Li'l Loc got out of the car and tossed both of their guns in. They both felt a big weight lift off of their shoulders as they rode on to the Hill.

About twenty minutes later they pulled up in front of the address that Grams gave them and parked behind two Denali trucks on spinners.

"I wonder whose trucks these are?" Li'l Loc said while getting out of the car.

Arab admired both of the cars for a brief second. "Whoever they belong to, the niggas must be paid," he said before turning around to walk up the steps.

*   *   *   *   *

Pretty Boy and his homies were inside their spot watching the surveillance monitors while smoking dro.

"Yo, who the fuck is that?" Bay Boe asked seeing the niggas out front looking at their whips.

"Looks like some crabs," Mr. Boo said picking his AK up from the floor.

The rest of the homies grabbed their guns as well, thinking that it was the North Side niggas that they had been feuding with for the past week.

"Hold up, that's my brother," Pretty Boy said noticing Li'l Loc and Arab on the monitors. Before they could get up the steps, he opened the door. "What ya'll doing on this side of town?" he asked smiling.

"Looking for you, nigga," Li'l Loc replied walking past Pretty Boy into the house with Arab following him.

When they entered the living room, their mouths dropped at the sight of all the guns laying around. Then when they looked up from the guns, they caught another surprise. Everybody in the house was dressed in red.

"What you doing with these slob-ass niggas, cuz?" Li'l Loc asked mean-mugging everybody in the living room.

"Ain't no slobs in here," Bay Boe said jumping up from the couch with his gun in hand.

"Be cool," Pretty Boy said getting in between them. "This is my brother CJ and my homie Arab. Arab and CJ, this is my homie Bay Boe."

"They call me Li'l Loc now, cuz," CJ said trying to relax a little while letting Pretty Boy know that things had changed since he moved.

"Well, they call me Pretty Boy over here," Brandon said letting him know that things had changed for him, too.

"So this is your family?" Bay Boe asked still clutching the MAC in his hands.

"Yes, this is my family."

"Well, any family of yours is my family as well," Bay Boe said putting his gun away.

Snype got up from the couch and passed Li'l Loc the blunt of dro that he was smoking to let him know that it was all love.

Li'l Loc and Arab sat on the couch and were introduced to the rest of the Bloods in the house.

After dapping everybody up, Li'l Loc sat back and shook his head smiling.

"What's you smiling about?" Pretty Boy asked him.

"You over here Blood'n getting' money, and I thought I was doing something."

"Them ya'll trucks out front?" Arab asked.

"Yea, we just got them last week," Mr. Boo answered.

"Forget the small talk . . . what we going to do about this nigga CK Black?" Li'l Loc asked.

"We already in with him, so it's going to be a piece of cake," Bay Boe said ready to ride.

"So how ya'll going to play it?" Arab asked.

"Me and Bay Boe going to hook up with him like we trying to re-up. While we inside, ya'll going to come up the back of the projects through this little trail that they got. The trail leads from the bottom to the top of the projects where CK Black's stash house is."

"It's going to be you, Arab, Snype, Bundy and LK on the trail, posted so when we come out, ya'll could back his nigga. Mr. Boo, you got to stay in the van and make sure you keep it running so we can get the fuck out of there ASAP Just remember that when them niggas hear the shots coming from the house, they going to be on us."

"What if the police come while ya'll in the spot? How am I going to be able to warn ya'll?" Mr. Boo asked.

"We going to take the walkie-talkies. Matter of fact, as soon as we see the coke, we going to put a few hot ones in him, then we going to hit ya'll after we pack up the coke," Pretty Boy answered.

"Everybody know their positions?" Bay Boe asked after Pretty Boy got done running the plan.

They all stated that they knew what to do, so Bay Boe picked up the phone and called CK Black, who answered after the second ring.

"What it be like?"

"This is your young Hill nigga, and I need to holler at you."

"Just come through," CK said before hanging up the phone.

"We on," Bay Boe told everybody.

"LK, we need you to go get us a mini van," Pretty Boy said.

"I'm on it," he replied before leaving the house.

"We going to need some guns," Li'l Loc said referring to himself and Arab.

"Take whatever ya'll need," Bay Boe said pointing to the guns on the floor.

About twenty minutes later, LK pulled up in front of the house.

"Call Mr. Ray and tell him we need a ride," Pretty Boy told Bay Boe.

Bay Boe called him and he answered after a few rings. He let him know that he needed to make a trip to Garfield and Mr. Ray told him that he would be on his way, so they sat back and waited.

"So what you going to do about that warrant?" Li'l Loc asked Pretty Boy.

"How you know about that?"

"Nigga, you on the news. Everybody know about it," Li'l Loc told him.

"I might turn myself in after we handle this CK Black situation," he said not wanting to be on the run for the rest of his life.

"You need to come back to Homewood and hide out with me and Arab."

"We seen the camera footage and you can definitely tell that it was you going in that bathroom," Arab said giving him even more reason not to turn himself in.

Before they could get into it any further, Bay Boe spoke up changing the subject so everybody could be focused on the task at hand. "Ya'll got to go change clothes," he told Li'l Loc and Arab.

"Change clothes for what?" Arab asked.

"If one of them Columbo niggas see ya'll with all that blue on, ya'll won't make it where ya'll need to be," Bay Boe explained.

"So what we going to wear?" Li'l Loc asked.

Bay Boe went upstairs to his room and grabbed two all-red Dickie suits for them to throw on. He went back downstairs and handed them the outfits, and Arab almost had a heart attack.

"Hell, nah, cuz . . . I ain't wearing that shit," Arab said looking at all the red.

"If this is the only way, then we got to put it on," Li'l Loc said changing his clothes.

Arab knew that he was right, so he followed suit.

As soon as they were dressed, Mr. Ray pulled up out front and began beeping his horn. "Let's do this," they said filing out of the house.

Bay Boe and Pretty Boy both had fully automatic fifty-shot MAC-10s with extra clips and a duffle bag filled with phone books. The rest of the squad had hundred-round AKs, so they were more than ready. Bay Boe got in the car with Mr. Ray and the rest of them got into the mini van.

"We going to the same place as usual, but this time we going to get back on our own," Bay Boe said paying him for the ride.

They knew that this might be their last ride, but they didn't care because they would be riding together.

When they got to the bottom of Columbo Street, Mr. Boo pulled the van over, while Mr. Ray continued driving to the top of the hill.

"Here you go, boss," Mr. Ray said pulling over in front of CK's stash house.

They thanked Mr. Ray and got out of the car with their hands on their guns.

As they were walking away from the car, Mr. Ray got on the phone and called the police.

"911 . . . how may I help you?"

"The kid who killed the guy at the movies live at 12 Roberts Street," he said giving the operator his info so he could receive the thousand dollar reward.

Bay Boe and Pretty Boy walked through the crowd of Bloods ready to do what they came to do. As they approached the front door, CK Black's girl opened it and ushered them in. "He's in the kitchen," she said pointing towards the back of the house.

They walked to the kitchen where CK was cooking up some work and greeted him same as they always did.

"What it be like?" CK asked them.

"We good," they both replied sitting down at the dining room table.

"I thought ya'll niggas would be laying low," CK said taking the crack out of the Pyrex and setting it on a paper towel.

"Laying low for what?" Bay Boe asked as CK walked into the dining room to handle his business.

"Pretty Boy's face been all over the news. What . . . ya'll ain't seen it?" he asked them.

"I ain't worried about that shit. I wasn't even at the movies last Friday," Pretty Boy said defending himself.

CK knew that he was lying because he saw the camera footage, and you could tell it was him entering the bathroom and, even though he had a bandana on his face when he left, you could still tell it was him leaving the bathroom with a gun in his hand. He decided to just leave it alone and get down to business, but first he remembered he had been wanting to tell Pretty Boy something about his chain.

"Pretty Boy, I finally remember who had a chain like yours," he said changing the subject.

"Who was it?" Pretty Boy asked.

"It was this one nigga name Loco from Homewood that I got into it with a long time ago."

"Oh, yeah," Pretty Boy said tensing up at the mention of his father's name.

"Yeah, him and his bitch-ass homies tried to test me when I first started getting money."

"What you do to them?" Pretty Boy asked wanting to hear CK admit to killing his dad.

"I handled them niggas accordingly," he replied grinning. The more he remembered about the story, the more he started to realize that Pretty Boy looked like Loco.

Bay Boe sat on the side of Pretty Boy, waiting for him to make his move.

"You know what, Blood?" CK said pointing at Pretty Boy.

"What's up?" Pretty Boy said fighting back tears.

"You kind of look like the bitch-ass nigga Loco," CK said thinking it was purely coincidental.

It was then that Pretty Boy pulled out his MAC-10 and put it in CK Black's face.

"What the fuck is you doing?"

"Loco was my dad and I am my father's son," Pretty Boy said sending a burst of rounds into CK Black's face.

Pretty Boy continued to let off bullets into Ck Black's lifeless body until the clip was empty.

"That's enough, dog," Bay Boe said grabbing his hand. Then he remembered that CK Black's girl was still in the house, so he ran into the living room to try and grab her, but he was too late. She was no where in sight, and he knew that she must have run out of the house to warn CK's goons. *Fuck*, he said to himself before running back into the dining room.

Pretty Boy was loading birds from the drop ceiling into the duffle bag that they had brought with them.

Bay Boe knew that there had to be more work in the house, so he told Pretty Boy to watch the door while he went upstairs to check the bedroom. Once upstairs, he went straight to the closet and the first thing he saw was a black duffle bag. He opened the bag and his eyes grew wide. "Jackpot," he said taking the bag and going downstairs.

As soon as Bay Boe came downstairs with the work, they headed to the front door to make their escape. But before they could open it up, bullets began tearing through the door and windows, causing them to hit the floor.

"Ya'll need to hurry the fuck up," Snype screamed into his walkie-talkie.

"We trapped in the fucking house," Bay Boe answered, getting up and running to the back door with Pretty Boy letting off rounds behind them just in case somebody decided to enter through the front.

As soon as they exited the house through the back, they began taking gunfire from CK Black's homies.

"Fuck ya'll niggas," Pretty Boy screamed while returning gunfire from his fully automatic MAC.

Bay Boe was letting off with his MAC as well and together they were backing down CK Black's goons. When they got to the back trail, they met up with the rest of their homies who all had their AKs blazin'.

They let off round after round while running down the hill to the waiting van. The doors were already open, and Bundy stood by the door letting off cover fire as everybody got in. Once the last person was inside, he turned around to get in behind them.

The Columbo niggas were still shooting and one of the bullets hit Bundy in the back and grazed his head. "I'm hit!" he hollered flying to the floor of the van.

Snype and LK aimed their choppers out the sliding door and began to spray rounds as Mr. Boo hit the gas.

"We got to get Bundy to the hospital," Bay Boe said looking at all the blood on the floor.

Everybody sat silent as Mr. Boo put the pedal to the metal, trying to get them back to the Hill as quick as possible.

Ten minutes later they pulled up in front of Bay Boe's house and he, Pretty Boy, Li'l Loc, Arab, and LK hopped out of the van, pulling Bundy out with them.

"Get rid of the van and the guns," Bay Boe said as Snype got in the passenger seat next to Mr. Boo.

"We got it," Mr. Boo said pulling off.

Arab, Li'l Loc and Pretty Boy went in the house while LK and Bay Boe grabbed the duffle bag and carried Bundy to the red Denali so they could get him to the hospital.

After getting in the truck, Bay Boe drove them to LK's house and dropped him off with the duffle bag full of coke.

"Be safe, Ike," LK said before getting out.

Bay Boe then sped to the hospital, hoping that his homie would be alright. "We almost there," he told Bundy who was laying motionless on the back seat.

CHAPTER 22

Pretty Boy, Li'l Loc and Arab were sitting in Bay Boe's spot, laying low after leaving a gang of bodies in the Columbo projects. As they passed blunts back and forth, their eyes were glued to the surveillance monitors so they could be on point at the first sign of trouble.

"Did ya'll get that nigga?" Li'l Loc asked breaking the silence.

"Yeah, we got him. I emptied my whole clip in his bitch ass."

"We need to stash all these guns somewhere, just in case the police hit," Arab said looking at all the guns on the floor.

"I got a little spot in the basement," Pretty Boy said picking the guns up and taking them downstairs to put in their stash spot.

When he came back up, Li'l Loc handed him a lit dutchee.

"We should be good," he told them in between puffs.

After about ten minutes of sitting on the couch smoking, Arab noticed some movement on the surveillance monitors. He looked closer trying to make sure the weed wasn't playing tricks on him. "Oh, shit, it's the police," he said jumping up from the couch.

Boom . . . boom . . . boom . . . boom came the loud knock at the door. "It's the Pittsburgh Police. Open up. We got the house surrounded."

"What we going to do?" Li'l Loc asked Pretty Boy hoping that he had an escape route for them or some type of plan.

*   *   *   *   *

Bay Boe pulled up at the emergency room and jumped out of the truck. He then went to the back door and helped his homie Bundy out. Bundy was half unconscious. "Come on, dog," Bay Boe said carrying him into the emergency room.

"I need some help!" he screamed walking up to the receptionist's desk.

After the receptionist made a call, the doctors rushed out and lifted Bundy onto a hospital bed before rushing him to surgery.

When he saw that Bundy was going to be alright, he went out side and got back into his truck to go meet up with Pretty Boy.

When he got to Roberts Street, he spotted a bunch of cop cars in front of his house. "What the fuck is going on?" he said to himself. After pulling over on the corner and getting out, the cops began screaming through the bullhorn.

"We have the house surrounded. Come out with your hands up."

He saw that there was nothing he could do, so he hopped back in the truck and drove around the corner to LK's house. He did not know if the police were watching LK's spot, so he parked around the corner form his house and walked the rest of the way.

When he got to his homie's spot, he began to knock frantically. LK opened up the door and ushered Bay Boe into the house, looking around to make sure there were no cops in sight.

"They got my spot surrounded," Bay Boe said sitting down on the couch.

"It's all over the news," LK said pointing to the television.

"*Man wanted for murder at Loew's theatre sought at 12 Roberts Street . . . Reporting to you live,*" the news reporter said.

"I thought they was looking for us about the Columbo shootout," Bay Boe said relieved but still worried for his homie.

*   *   *   *   *

"Come out with your hands up or we're going to kick the door in!" the police hollered through the bullhorn once again.

Pretty Boy looked at the surveillance monitors and saw the Swat team getting ready to break the door down.

"We ain't got no choice, but to go out there," Li'l Loc said ready to give up.

They knew that the police weren't there about the Columbo shootout because they had the news on, but they were still worried about Brandon and all the guns stashed in the basement.

"If we don't go out there, they just going to kick the door in anyway," Arab said agreeing with Li'l Loc.

Pretty Boy knew that they were right, so he opened the door and walked out of the house with his hands up. Li'l Loc and Arab followed behind him, doing the same.

As soon as they were out of the house, the police swarmed them. "Brandon Myers, you are under arrest for the murder of Mark Johnson," they said cuffing him.

None of them said a word, honoring the code of the streets which was silence.

As they were putting them in the back of the paddy wagon, Snype and Mr. Boo came around the corner from duping the guns and van. They saw what was gong on and they left as fast as they came.

The police searched the house for the murder weapon, but didn't find anything, and then they transported them to the homicide precinct on the East Side. After five hours of interrogation, they were standing strong, all of them holding water. The only words that any of them said were, "I want to see my lawyer."

The detectives let Li'l Loc and Arab go because they didn't have anything on them, but they had the video footage of Pretty Boy, so he didn't have a chance. After letting his brother and homie go, they tried to question him one more time.

"So what did you do with the gun?" the detective asked him.

"I don't know what the fuck you talking about," Pretty Boy replied.

"Okay, tough guy, we're going to see how tough you are in the state prison system when some grown man is punkin' you."

"Fuck you, bitch-ass cop" Pretty Boy said spitting in the detective's face.

They saw that Pretty Boy was unbreakable, so they transferred him to the Allegheny County Jail and put him on the block with all the other juveniles who were being charged as adults.

They had him in isolation for a week, but once he signed a waver that said he didn't want to be housed in protective custody, he was allowed in the general population.

The first thing he did was call Grams to let her know his situation. After telling her that he was being charged with a homicide, she broke down and cried for the rest of the phone call. She felt that it was her fault that he was in jail because it had been her idea to move from Homewood to the Hill.

The next day while he was playing cards, the guard called his name for a visit. He went upstairs to the visiting room and sat down behind the double windows separating him from Grams. To his surprise Ki-Ki was also there, and he smiled from ear to ear when he saw her.

"How you doing in there?" Grams asked with tears in her eyes.

"I'm fine," he replied trying to maintain his composure. He hated to put Grams through the bullshit, but there was nothing she or anyone else could have done to prevent him from being in the streets. The street life was in his blood.

He and Grams talked for fifteen minutes before she stepped out to give him and Ki-Ki some privacy.

"So what up?" Pretty Boy asked smiling at how good she looked.

"I'm not doing too good," she replied with sadness in he voice.

"What's wrong?"

For a few seconds she was silent, then she burst out crying. "I'm pregnant," she said wishing that he was on the other side of the glass with her.

His heart dropped at the thought of becoming a father. "So you going to keep it?" he asked her.

"Yes," she replied not knowing how she was going to be both Mommy and Daddy to their child.

For the rest of the visit, they all discussed what they could do for the baby if he didn't get out soon.

Pretty Boy explained that he might be able to get decertified and then the most he would get was juvenile life. This meant that he would be locked up until his twenty-first birthday. He was going on seventeen, so he would only have to do four years and some change.

He also told Grams about the money that he had in his stash, and she promised to use the money to take care of Ki-Ki, his child, and him until he came home.

"I almost forgot to tell you that I seen Bay Boe and Li'l Loc and they told me to tell you that they got fifty birds off CK Black, and they promised they would get at you whenever things cooled down."

"Tell them I said to be safe and let them know that I'm aiight down here," he told her before she and Grams left.

He had seen the Columbo shootout on the news, and he knew that the police didn't have any witnesses. After all that he had been through, he had a lot on his mind, but his last though before going to sleep was, *Damn, I'm going to be a father*.

CHAPTER 23

Pretty Boy did a month in the County jail before being decertified and transferred to the juvenile detention center. He spent five months there waiting to go to court for voluntary manslaughter, which is what he was charged with since the three surviving victims all testified that Pretty Boy had been defending himself when he killed their friend.

Today was his court day and he was nervous as hell. Even though he would more than likely get juvenile life, he was hoping to catch a break. As he sat in the holding cell—which was known as the sweat box because of the blasting heat and the lack of ventilation—he thought about Ki-Ki.

The last time he had seen her, she was big as a house. His homies had given her another message to pass on, letting him know they were back in mode. Bay Boe had a new spot in the hood jumpin' and Li'l Loc and Arab had a spot in Homewood on lock. They also told her to tell him that they had some change for him.

Two weeks later they dropped off two hundred fifty thousand dollars at his grams' house, and he told her to put the money up and continue to use the eighty thousand to support him, Ki-Ki and herself. It was a big relief that his family would be alright financially so he wouldn't have to worry so much about them, but he would miss them while he was away.

"Brandon Myers," the guard called out interrupting his thoughts.

"That's me," he said walking to the door.

"It's your time to go in front of the judge," the guard said putting the shackles and cuffs on him.

As he walked to the court room, he braced himself for what was to come. When he entered the room, he noticed his homies sitting in the back. He was hoping they were going to be there and he smiled at their show of support. Even his homie Bundy was there, and this made him smile because the last time he saw him, he didn't look like he would make it.

Seeing his family made him feel a lot better about the situation he was in and he stood tall, ready to take whatever the judge dished out.

"So, Mr. Brandon Myers, how are you today?" the judge asked as if he really gave a fuck.

"I'm doing aiight," he replied playing his little game.

"So, counsel, what are we going to do with your client today?"

"First, your Honor, I want you to know that my client is a straight A student and he had no prior record. He is in all honor classes at Brashear High School, and he is also an excellent role model."

The judge had heard this same story many times before and he cut the attorney off in mid-sentence. "What you're telling me sounds real good, but your client committed a heinous crime and the only reason he was decertified is because the victims testified that your client didn't start the altercation, which I sincerely doubt is the truth. But even if it is true, it still doesn't hide the fact that your client killed a man and wounded several others. For this reason, I am going to sentence him to juvenile life in New Castle Maximum Prison."

Pretty Boy didn't even flinch when he was sentenced because he was prepared for the worst.

"Mr. Brandon Myers, do you have anything that you want to say?" the judge asked him.

"No, your Honor," he replied knowing that no matter what he said, it wouldn't change the judge's mind.

"Take this man away," the judge told the sheriff, who was standing in the background just in case Pretty Boy tried to run.

After being cuffed, he turned around and walked towards the door amidst words of encouragement from his friends and family.

"Keep your head up, Ike," LK told him.

"Be strong, Blood," Bundy said.

"We got you, dog," Mr. Boo told him.

Arab and Snype told him the same as everyone else, letting him know that they would be there for him.

"We going to be out here waiting for you," Bay Boe said holding back tears. He and Pretty Boy had gotten really close over the past few months and he felt like he was losing a brother.

"I love you, baby," Ki-Ki told him with tears in her eyes. She was hurting because she wouldn't have him by her side to help raise their son for the next four years. She was just another single black mother.

"Whenever you get back to the jail, call me so I can come visit before they transfer you," Grams said giving him a hug.

Before he left the court room, Li'l Loc stood up with tears in his eyes. He and Pretty Boy had come a long way—not only did they live the dream they both shared, they also killed the person responsible for the murder of their fathers. "Yo, Pretty Boy," he said getting his brother's attention.

When Pretty Boy looked back at him, he asked, "Am I my brother's keeper?"

Even though they were affiliated with different gangs that had a long-time rivalry with each other, they still stood strong as brothers, displaying their love for each other while avenging the death of their fathers. Their actions showed that the brotherly bond they shared was stronger than their ties to any gang.

"Yes, I am my brother's keeper," Pretty Boy answered before leaving the court room.

EPILOGUE

Pretty Boy put on his best thousand-yard stare as he walked through the New Castle Max recreation yard. He was fresh off the bus and he didn't know what to expect from the prisoners already there. His homie in the detention center told him that it was a rough place, and from the look of the niggas lifting weights, he could tell that he would have to get his weight up quickly if he wanted to make it back home alive.

"Keep it moving," the guard said nudging him along.

He had stopped to look at his surroundings and had forgotten that the guards were even there to escort him. That's how nervous he was. The guard walked him to the intake area where he was stripped, searched, showered and processed into the jail's system. By now the nervousness had worn off and he was ready for whatever came his way.

"Pick up your stuff and come on," the guard told him once he was done with the intake process. He led Pretty Boy to the living quarters. There was nothing there but cells and a few tables on the compound where a few inmates were playing chess and cards. Everybody stared at him as he passed and he stared right back, not wanting to look like a punk by backing down from them.

"This is you right here," the guard said standing in front of what would be his new home for the next five years. He opened the door and moved to the side so Pretty Boy could step in. Once he was inside, the door was slammed shut behind him.

For a while the whole process had felt like a dream to Pretty Boy, but the sound of the door made it all reality. As soon as he was in the cell, he noticed a kid sitting at the writing desk reading a book. He dropped his personal belongings to the floor and stood ready for a confrontation.

"Yo, cuz, where you from?" the guy asked standing up from the desk. He said "cuz" so Pretty Boy knew he was more than likely from Pittsburgh.

Pretty Boy looked the guy up and down. He was dark skinned with braids and about the same height as Pretty Boy, but he was a lot wider and you could tell that he had been lifting weights for a long while. Then he looked down at the man's shoes. In jail, you could tell by a guy's shoes where he was from or what he claimed, and the money-green, grey and white Air Maxes that the guy had on let Pretty Boy know that he was probably a Westgate Convict.

His set didn't really have any problems with the Convicts, so he loosened up a bit. "I'm from the Hill and I rep Bedford Avenue Bloods," Pretty Boy told him.

"Well, I'm from Westgate and I claim Convict," the guy told him.

"So what do you go by?" Pretty Boy asked.

"They call me H," the kid replied.

"They call me Pretty Boy." He was relaxed and it seemed that H was a slight dude, but it was too early to tell. He wondered what H stood for anyway, but it was too early to be asking a whole bunch of personal questions.

"So what's it like up here?" Pretty Boy asked while setting up his property and claiming his space.

"It's real laid back for the most part. It don't really be no gang violence because up here Pittsburgh niggas stick together," he explained to him.

This was all good with Pretty Boy, because he was trying to avoid getting into the bullshit. He had money and his son to get back to and he wasn't trying to let anything get in between that.

After Pretty Boy unpacked his stuff, he laid down on his bed and drifted off to sleep.

*   *   *   *   *

Pretty Boy had been incarcerated at New Castle Max for a week and things were going smoothly. It seemed that H pretty much ran the facility, and since he was his roommate, nobody bothered him. They had weed and cigarettes, and H could get liquor if he wanted it. It felt like he was still on the streets.

"Yo, H, I don't want you to think that I'm in your business, but what do H mean?" They were sitting in the cell smoking a joint when Pretty Boy asked this question.

"Heroin," H replied with a smile on his face.

"You mean like the drug?" Pretty Boy asked.

"Yes. Heroin like the drug," H replied.

"So that's really your real name?" Pretty Boy asked. He didn't think it was because the guards all called him Quincy.

"Yep, Heroin is my first name, but I go by my middle name to everybody who is not in the game. My uncle was a big-time drug dealer and he gave me the name," H explained.

"I feel you, dog," Pretty Boy said lying down in his bunk.

H hopped up on his bed, and for a second there was silence between them.

"So, Pretty Boy, what was you into out there?" H asked after deciding in his head that Pretty Boy was an alright dude.

"I use to move a little bit of coke out there," he replied being modest. He didn't want to brag about all the work he moved, because he didn't yet trust H one hundred per cent. "What about you?" he asked wondering what type of shit he was into on the streets. He could tell that H was getting some money because he carried himself as if he was a boss on the outside and he also made moves like one.

H was silent for a second, and then he looked down at Pretty Boy with a grin. "I move that heroin."

The way he said it made Pretty Boy feel like it was a privilege to be in the cell with H and he knew that nothing but good would come out of it. He had always heard the saying *There is no money like dope money* and he was eager to learn about H's success in the heroin business. So even though they had only been friends for a short while, Pretty Boy jumped off the limb and asked a simple question that would open the door to a whole new life: "What was the dope game like?"

To be continued.........

ABOUT THE AUTHOR

N. C. Manuel is an up-and-coming author who grew up on the mean streets of the Hill District, one of the most notorious communities in Pittsburgh, Pennsylvania. He began writing while serving a eleven year prison sentence. He is now a self -published author and full time student at CCAC pursuing a Associates Degree in Business Management

Despite facing all types of adversity, he is determined to rise above the streets and become successful in the book game.

My Brother's Keeper is the first book of a planned trilogy.

If you like 'My Brother's Keeper' check out 'Destiny's Intertwined' which is the prequel to the next release in the 'My Brothers' series and 'My Brothers Revenge'!

TO CONTACT AUTHOR N.C. MANUEL GO TO ONE OF THE FOLLOWING:

www.facebook.com/BayBoe
Instagram.com/LoveandLoyaltyPublications
LoveandLoyaltypub@gmail.com
Authorncmanuel.blogspot.com

BOOKS AVAILABLE ON AMAZON.COM/KINDLE MY BROTHERS KEEPER WEB SERIES COMING SOON!!!! 2017!!!

ALSO CHECK OUT BETRAYED BY LOVE!

BETRAYED BY LOVE 2 (BACHELORETTE PARTY) coming soon!!!!